DRAGON DANCE

THE FIREBALL TRILOGY

DRAGON DANCE

BOOK THREE

JOHN CHRISTOPHER

Aladdin

New York   London   Toronto   Sydney   New Delhi

This book is a work of fiction. Any references to historical events, real people, or real places are used fictitiously. Other names, characters, places, and events are products of the author's imagination, and any resemblance to actual events or places or persons, living or dead, is entirely coincidental.

ALADDIN

An imprint of Simon & Schuster Children's Publishing Division
1230 Avenue of the Americas, New York, New York 10020
This Aladdin paperback edition October 2015
Text copyright © 1986 by John Christopher
Previously published in 1986 by E.P. Dutton.
Cover illustration copyright © 2015 by Anton Petrov
Also available in an Aladdin hardcover edition.

For information about special discounts for bulk purchases, please contact
Simon & Schuster Special Sales at 1-866-506-1949 or business@simonandschuster.com.
The Simon & Schuster Speakers Bureau can bring authors to your live event. For more information or to book an event contact the Simon & Schuster Speakers Bureau at 1-866-248-3049 or visit our website at www.simonspeakers.com.
Cover designed by Karin Paprocki
Interior designed by Hilary Zarycky
The text of this book was set in Venetian 301.
Manufactured in the United States of America 0915 OFF
2 4 6 8 10 9 7 5 3 1
Library of Congress Control Number 2014948955
ISBN 978-1-4814-2016-7 (hc)
ISBN 978-1-4814-2015-0 (pbk)
ISBN 978-1-4814-2017-4 (eBook)

to C. de P. jnr

I

AS THEY HEADED OUT, THE WHITE mist thinned and finally went; it still hid the shore, but otherwise visibility was good. In fact, there wasn't anything to see but water, stretching blue and unbroken north and south, and westwards to the horizon. The breeze had stiffened, and the sea became choppy. This was an unwieldy vessel, more raft than boat, made up of half a dozen dugout hulls lashed together beneath a bamboo deck. It rolled heavily, and several of the Indians were sick, in a businesslike fashion, over the side. Simon repressed an urge to follow their example.

Brad was looking his usual imperturbable self.

The morning was warm, a sign that spring was well advanced. Not that the winter in coastal California had been severe, but there had been plenty of damp miserable days in which he had been glad of the shelter of the palm-thatched Indian hut. It was surprising, he thought, how one got used to things—smells, for instance.

He asked Brad: "What kind of fish, do you think?"

The Indians were used to the pale-skinned strangers talking in their unintelligible tongue, and the remark aroused no interest. Brad shrugged.

"From the length of the poles, I'd guess something sizeable. Dolphin or tuna—perhaps swordfish. I hope not dolphin."

Simon, too, would once have been repelled by the idea of killing an intelligent creature for food, but that was a long way back. The thought of food of any kind at the moment, though, was nauseous. He said: "Do you still think it was a smart idea to come on this trip?"

"If we're hoping to become members of the tribe, it is."

This, of course, was the big question over which they had wrangled since reaching the Indian village, soaked and half-starved, a couple of months earlier. Despite that last remark, Brad had been in favour of moving on, Simon of staying. Brad always was in favour of moving on—an inclination which had carried them halfway round the world and led them into more hot spots than Simon cared to count.

It was not that he found the life of the tribe particularly attractive. Apart from the occasional hunt for antelope or red deer, the routine was basically one of idleness. The braves, when they were not kippering themselves in the smoke hut, occupied themselves with intricate basketwork, making feathered costumes and headdresses, and painting rocks—pursuits for which Simon and Brad lacked both skill and aptitude. They were also given to singing, especially late in the evening: songs which at best were long, incomprehensible, and boring. When the braves were high as a result of smoking dried thorn-apple flowers, the songs took on a wilder note, sometimes resulting in violent scuffles. After the first, they had steered clear of the thorn-apple parties—all Simon got out of the one pipe he tried was a blinding headache.

All the same, he favoured staying put, at least for the time being, and Brad had reluctantly agreed. The tribe provided food, shelter, and protection from external hazards, advantages which past experience had taught him to value highly. There was in fact a good case to be argued for remaining with the tribe permanently, provided this was permitted, and Simon had argued it. That argument had been inconclusive. It would probably be renewed with the coming of summer. Meanwhile it made sense to go along with the tribe's way of life.

Night Eagle began rapping out commands. He was the chief, an Indian of above-average height with unchallenged authority over the rest of the braves. That authority was much more dubious where his chief wife, Little Green Bird, was concerned. She was a small but ample lady, lavishly decked in bright cloths, feathered ornaments, and bone bangles, who was always capable of putting a worried look on her husband's normally impassive countenance. She had an affectionate nature, and had taken a fancy to Brad. Her fondness for embracing him partly accounted for his eagerness to move on.

The bamboo poles, between ten and fifteen feet

in length, carried long lines fitted with large barbless bone hooks, on which the braves now impaled chunks of unsavoury-looking meat. They came from an antelope carcass so rotten that even the village dogs had turned up their noses at it.

Once the hooks were baited, Night Eagle cast the lines from three poles in turn, handing each pole over to a pair of braves who slotted the end into a hole recessed in the deck. It was obviously customary for the chief to make the cast—though it didn't seem to involve any great skill—and Simon and Brad kept well out of the way while this was going on. They had learned the importance of ritual in Indian life, and how easy it was to offend against it unwittingly.

A member of the tribe who would not be at all sorry to see them land in trouble was Night Eagle's son, Stone Blade. He was perhaps a year younger than they were, and had shown his dislike for the two strangers. Especially for Brad, which could be connected with his mother's partiality for him. Stone Blade had been moved out of the women's quarters to live with the braves a few days after their arrival, which probably made things worse.

Watching proceedings beside Simon in the stern, Brad said: "I don't see two men holding a really big one."

Brad's habit of sounding knowledgeable about everything could still rile Simon, and seasickness did not help. He said: "I suppose deep-sea fishing was another of those sports you practised back home?"

Brad shook his head. "No, but it stands to reason. A big tuna can weigh as much as two thousand pounds."

Before Simon could respond to that, a cry went up from one of the braves. The deck lurched, and the line tautened towards a point on the port bow. A large hump rose, then resubmerged. The boat veered in that direction.

Simon immediately appreciated Brad's point. The bamboo pole bent into a shallow arc across the gunnel: so strong was the pull that the two men were bound to be plucked from their footing into the sea.

But something else happened before that. With ecstatic whoops, the Indians threw themselves onto the pole holders, securing themselves with hands and feet, fingers and toes, to the rocking deck. The boat sped on in the wake of the great fish. Simon and Brad had to dig in hard themselves to avoid going overboard.

"You didn't think of that one," Simon gasped.

"It'll be all right as long as . . ."

Brad didn't finish the sentence. The boat tilted sharply, banging them against the deck again. Clouds spun across the sky, and Simon had terrifying glimpses of a shifting horizon and menacing sea. Then there was a shout from Night Eagle, and sea and horizon spun back to where they had been. The boat hit the water with a bang, and a splash that drenched them all.

It wasn't difficult to work out what had happened. The tuna had dived, threatening to capsize the boat, and the chief had taken emergency action. As he got to his feet, Simon saw Night Eagle replacing his knife—an obsidian blade traded from Indians of the interior—in its deerskin and bone sheath. The severed line dangled from its pole.

The Indians seemed to take the setback philosophically. As Brad suggested, it must be a not uncommon occurrence. He went on: "They could play the fish better with a longer line."

"You tell Night Eagle," Simon said. "I'm sure he'd appreciate being clued up on tribal skills by a visiting paleface. Bearing in mind tensile strength might have something to do with it."

"Something in that," Brad admitted. "I was thinking in terms of stuff like nylon. Coyote hair, even well plaited, doesn't really match up."

The Indians had resumed tossing out ground bait. Simon felt a little better. The near capsizing of the boat, though alarming, seemed to have settled his stomach. And it was satisfying to have put Brad right about something.

There was a second bite within quarter of an hour, followed by the same procedure of the other Indians piling on top of the pole holders. But the initial shock was not so great this time, and the boat was hauled less swiftly through the water. A couple of times it tilted, but righted itself.

Eventually Simon thought he detected a slowing in the pace. Soon after, on a command from Night Eagle, two braves detached themselves. The gunnels carried struts with transverse crosspieces, and as the line fractionally slackened they hooked it onto one of them and went on winding it round, hauling in the tiring fish.

It finally broke water, revealing itself as close on seven feet in length, yellow finned, with a golden stripe down one side. It was pulled close in, and

Night Eagle leaned out, stabbing with his obsidian knife. Blood spurted, and the tuna heaved convulsively. He stabbed again, and the braves got together to drag it inboard.

Simon was standing close by, watching. Too close: a sudden impact of slimy wetness sent him sprawling. He heard a splash and thought the fish might have slipped back, but got up to see it still writhing on the deck. But Brad was missing.

He was in the water, several feet from the boat with the gap increasing. The Indians, preoccupied with the tuna, were paying no heed to him. Simon dived in.

Closing on him, he asked: "You okay?"

"Don't waste your breath. Swim."

The gap had increased; the boat's primitive leather sail was filled with a strong southeasterly breeze. Simon called out, trying to attract the attention of the Indians.

Brad gasped: "Swim!"

They were making no progress—in fact, losing ground. One of the Indians at least was aware of their problem: Stone Blade had abandoned the fish to stare in their direction. Even at this distance, Simon could see the grin on his face.

He swam doggedly. He didn't know how far from shore they were, but guessed at least ten miles. He tried to recall the longest distance he had swum—a mile, maybe, in the school swimming pool? And would the Indians really abandon them? He had a nasty suspicion about the answer.

As the gap went on widening, he felt himself starting to flag. Their lives over the last couple of years had been strenuous, but strenuous on dry land. Swimming used different muscles, and theirs were out of condition.

The boat was more than fifty yards distant when Night Eagle at last looked towards them, and issued a command. The sail was brought about in the primitive tacking operation the Indians used. It lost the wind, and the boat idled while they slogged their way towards it.

The Indians offered no help as Brad and Simon dragged themselves on board. They had turned back to the tuna, and were skinning and dividing it.

When they had their breaths back, Brad said: "Thanks. You shouldn't have come in after me, though."

From a practical point of view, that was probably true. Brad was the stronger swimmer, and it was unlikely that the sight of two swimming for their lives rather than one would have influenced Night Eagle. Simon said: "There'd have been no need if you hadn't let yourself get knocked overboard by the tuna."

"I was thinking that it might have been more useful to throw me a line. And it wasn't the fish that sent me over."

"What did, then?"

Brad nodded in the direction of Stone Blade. "Our little friend caught me off balance."

"Are you serious?"

"Yes. So was he."

Simon wondered if Night Eagle had seen that; he didn't miss much. He wondered, too, how close they had come to being abandoned. The Indians had received them with the usual hospitality that was offered to strangers in need, but strangers were expected to move on in due course. Acceptance as members of the tribe was something else; and presumably the final decision there was up to the chief.

Like his son, Night Eagle might have been resenting Little Green Bird's attentions to Brad. He'd shown nothing, but he never did. The time during which they were swimming desperately after the boat could have been one in which Night Eagle weighed the satisfaction of being rid of the palefaces against his wife's wrath when he returned without them.

Simon said: "This is something we ought to think a bit seriously about."

Brad nodded. "I'm doing that."

Course was set for home: the Indians plainly were satisfied with their catch. Justifiably so—there were a couple of hundred pounds of good meat on the carcass at least. There would be a feast that night.

The weather had stayed calm, and the coastal mist was still present, though increasingly patchy. It swirled about them, varying between thick grey fog and a tendriled whiteness touched with the sun's gold. They were heading south of east—their voyage had taken them a long way north of the village.

The mist continued to thin, and finally they could see the coastline. Brad gripped Simon's arm. The shore was a couple of hundred yards off, flat and featureless but for one thing: the crumbling outline of an unmistakably Chinese pagoda.

It was an edifice they had seen once before, when they reached the Pacific coast after trekking across the continent from the Gulf of Florida. They had even explored the ruin, finding nothing of interest, only dust and decay, before resuming the journey which took them to Night Eagle's village.

Simon said: "I suppose we could ask Night Eagle about it."

Brad, who as usual had been quicker at picking up the language, put a question to the chief. Simon didn't grasp the guttural response, but Night Eagle's normally expressionless face showed distaste, and maybe more.

He asked: "What did he say?"

"Bad spirits, bad people, bad something else. Definitely bad."

"Not much help, then. Not that it matters."

"No. I'm not sure. I'd very much like to know just how a thing like that ties in with the fireball."

The fireball had been the beginning of an adventure that had lasted two and a half years and taken them six thousand miles from their starting point. From Simon's, at least, because it happened while he was playing reluctant host to Brad, a hitherto unknown American cousin, on summer vacation in England. While out walking, they had encountered a shimmering white sphere of light, which Brad thought could be a fireball, a form of ball lightning. Going forward to take a closer look had resulted in the shattering and incredible experience of finding themselves sucked into it—and emerging into a world geographically identical with their own, yet frighteningly different.

They had gradually worked out a theory that explained what had happened. The fireball had been a crossing point between their world and one lying on a different probability track—an If world. It was a dizzying thought that there might be an infinite number of such worlds, invisibly side by side.

This particular world was one in which the Roman empire, instead of declining and falling, had retained its power and its control of Europe through to the twentieth century. Their arrival in it had proved, in fact, to be the means of breaking that power. Much had happened since, and here they were—still trying to adjust to this different pattern but now in an equally transformed southern California.

• • •

Although they did not mention their escape from drowning to Little Green Bird, one of the Indians must have: she scolded Brad for his carelessness while enfolding him in her ample bosom. The caresses continued until household duties connected with the impending feast took her attention elsewhere.

They went to the swimming hole below the village. While Brad was strenuously scrubbing himself, Simon said: "She obviously doesn't give a monkey's whether *I* get drowned. How do you do it, Brad?"

Brad contented himself with a filthy look. "I've had enough of this. Did you see Stone Blade's face while his mom was doing her hugging bit? Today was probably a spur-of-the-moment effort. Next time he'll plan things properly." Brad climbed out of the hole and rubbed himself with the coarse towel. "You stay if you like. I'm going."

"Right now?"

"If past form is anything to go by, the feast tonight will wind up with them all getting high on thorn apple. It'll be late tomorrow afternoon before they start taking notice again."

Simon nodded. "And that would give us time to get well clear. I don't suppose Night Eagle would be keen on sending out a search party, but Little Green Bird might make him. So, dawn tomorrow?"

"Yes. We can grab a few days' rations from the leftovers."

The feast began with speeches and long declamatory poems, continuing with songs to an accompaniment of an orchestra of rattles, whistles, and drums. If you had a taste for it, it probably sounded great. To Simon, it felt like having his eardrums sandblasted.

Things improved when the women started bringing food round—by now he was ravenously hungry. Little Green Bird attended to Brad personally, giving him the tastiest morsels together with pats and squeezes. The eating and drinking were punctuated by more songs and by dances. The shamans, their leader magnificently attired in a white deerskin and feather-and-pebble headdress, performed a special dance which ended with the passing round of the first of the pipes of glowing thorn apple. The pipe passed from the shamans to the chief, and then to the braves.

Simon wondered about their future. Even apart from Brad's special problems, he realized it would have been difficult, perhaps impossible, for them to become regular members of the tribe. To live the Indian life, you needed to have been Indian reared. Their backgrounds of twentieth-century English (or American, in Brad's case) just didn't fit.

But he thought too, and with a touch of resentment, about the fact that once again it was Brad making the big decision, himself simply acquiescing in it. When they first met, back in prefireball England, his cousin's cocksureness had incensed him. It had been satisfying when he had goaded Brad into fighting, and even more satisfying that his own greater physical strength was going to put the result beyond doubt. Brad, though, had refused to give in, and it had been he, in the end, who had offered the apology and stuck a hand out.

Since then, it seemed, although he had won a few minor conflicts, Brad's view had prevailed on all the major issues. Did this prove him the weaker character? He supposed it must. On the other hand, since Brad was not going to be swayed once he had made his mind up, it always seemed more rational to go

along with him. One thing certain about this peril-
ous world was that they were safer together than
apart. If they ever got back to their own world, Brad
could do whatever crazy thing he liked, and he would
wave him a more than cheerful good-bye. But that
was a bigger pipe dream than the one the braves were
working up to. There was no way back.

Brad nudged him.

"What?"

"I think it's getting to them. Four pipes in circu-
lation, and they're reaching the noisy stage. In half
an hour, they should start passing out."

There was a hush as the chief shaman began to
sing again, a wailing chant accompanied by peculiar
jerkings of his arms and feet. Outlined against the
light of the fire, his antics were bizarre—a comic
turn, though definitely not one to be laughed at,
especially with the braves high on thorn apple.

At that point, something even odder happened.
Simon heard a resonant bell-like sound, which only
slowly and tremblingly died away. And it did not
come from the firelit area, but from somewhere out
in the shadows. The shaman froze into an immo-
bility as weird as his dancing, and a strange sigh

gusted along the ranks of the squatting Indians.

This was something entirely new, and he wondered what it signified. He whispered to Brad: "What do you think?"

"Shh . . ."

From beyond the circle of firelight, figures approached. They wore cloaks over brightly coloured pantaloons, and one had what looked like a bronze helmet. They stooped over the motionless Indians and spoke to them. They were speaking in the Indians' tongue, but with strange accents.

"Obey!" Simon heard. "Be still—obey. . . ."

When they reached Brad and Simon, Simon realized something else: they were not Indians but Orientals.

A pair of hands grasped his head, and a voice addressed him: "Be still. Obey!"

After completing the circle of the braves, the newcomers moved away, towards the hut with the women and children. The Indians stayed as they had left them, unmoving.

Brad said quietly: "I don't know what this is, but I'm not crazy about it. Ready to go, while they're offstage?"

Simon nodded. There was a tight knot of fear in his belly. A few yards away, he saw Night Eagle, blindly staring into space. None of the Indians moved as they cautiously got up and made their way towards the trees. There was plenty of food lying about, but he was no longer concerned about rations for the journey. Getting away would be enough.

They came to the edge of the trees. He glanced towards Brad, and saw Brad turning to him with a look of warning.

Save it for later, he thought, and then thought nothing at all as something hit him, very heavily, behind the right ear.

2

SIMON WAS LYING BACK ON A RECLINING seat on the verandah of the tennis club. He felt tired, but pleasantly aware of having just won a hard set of mixed doubles, and with Lucy Gaines as his partner, too. The day was warm and bright, and he could hear the thump of ball on racket and distant voices. The only drawback to perfect happiness was thirst; and at his elbow stood a tall glass of iced lime juice and soda. He took a long swig from it.

Lucy Gaines was whispering in his ear, which would be very nice if he could make out what she was saying. He listened harder. Her voice was deeper than he remembered. What *was* she saying?

"Si! Wake up. Si . . ."

He didn't remember her ever calling him Si. But Brad did. In fact, that was Brad's voice. He opened his eyes, and the sunlit afternoon went. It was dark, with a smell of people and must and spices, and a creaking sound, and a hard surface rocking slightly beneath him. He croaked: "Brad . . ."

"Okay, buddy?"

"Thirsty . . ."

"Hang in there."

He tried to marshal his muzzy thoughts, but they slipped away from him. They were going to move on in the morning. . . . Little Green Bird wasn't going to like losing Brad. . . . The songs at the feast, the shaman's weird dance . . . He felt the swaying surface, heard the creaking. Suddenly he was alert. He was on a boat: it was unmistakable. But what about the feast?

He remembered the bell-like sound, the cloaked men moving among the Indians, he and Brad sneaking towards the trees. . . . Where was Brad? He swallowed with a dry throat. Although it was very dark, a lighter rectangle showed above, with a small point of brilliance inside it. A star, seen through an open hatch? He became aware again of the surrounding smell of people. But there was no snoring—no sound of breathing, for that matter.

Simon's head started thumping as he heaved himself into a sitting position. He put out a hand and felt cloth, then flesh. It was cold and unresponsive, and he recoiled instinctively. Was it a corpse? Was he surrounded by dead bodies?

Something obscured the hatch light, and there was the sound of feet on a ladder. He whispered: "Brad?"

"Here."

He felt a metal beaker being presented and drank water gratefully.

Brad said: "Sorry to be so long. I had to wait while one of the Chinese filled a bucket at the water tank."

"Chinese?"

"Okay, it sounds crazy—but we did find that pagoda. Perhaps in this world they spread east, across the Bering Strait. Perhaps they have a colony up north. In Washington, maybe, or British Columbia."

Simon's thoughts would not come together. "But what are they *doing*?"

"I'd think that's obvious. Slaving."

"The Indians, you mean? I touched one of them. I think they're dead."

"No, they're not dead. It's some kind of trance state. The gong probably started it off, followed by that business of holding heads and giving commands. They were already high on thorn apple. Maybe that's why it didn't work with us—we hadn't smoked any."

Simon reached out again and touched flesh.

"This one's really cold."

"And scarcely breathing. It's a deep trance. Blood pressure very low, too, I'd guess. If you pricked his arm, he'd ooze rather than bleed."

"I don't understand." Simon rubbed his aching head. "Did I get hit?"

"Yes, you got hit. I thought it made sense to pretend I was tranced, like the Indians. They had two of them carry you here."

"We're on a ship?"

"Yes. There were boats tied up at the creek the Indians use. I doubt it's the first time they've been here. Remember how Night Eagle reacted to the pagoda. We rowed out to this junk, and then the Indians were ordered into the hold and put back to sleep. I've been waiting for you to surface. I thought I might have to wait all night—or longer. I think it was a sandbag you got hit with."

Simon moved his head and groaned. "Some sand. How far offshore are we?"

"Maybe half a mile."

"We could swim that!"

"Yes. How do you feel about tackling the ladder?"

"Not happy, but it's better than the alternative. Where's the hatch? I can't see it now."

"The sky was clouding when I was on deck. Hang on to me."

Almost at once, Simon trod on someone. A leg rolled nauseously under his foot, but there was no outcry. He trod on others on the way to the ladder, two lines of rope with wooden rungs. He managed to follow Brad up it, despite a new wave of dizziness, and heaved himself on deck. It was scarcely less dark than below, with no stars or moonlight. A stiffish breeze was blowing. Onshore or off? He put it to Brad.

"I don't know. We came in over that bulwark there, but she could have swung on her anchor chain. In fact, she could have swung right round."

So was it half a mile to shore, or over five thousand? It made a difference.

"When it starts to get light . . ."

"Yes," Brad said. "Meanwhile we'd better take cover, in case one of the crew comes along. There's a pile of cargo amidships."

They found a coil of rope to sit on. The wind was freshening further, and there was an occasional drop of rain. Simon said, keeping his voice low: "You really think they're from the north?"

"They must be."

"You don't suppose? . . ."

"What?"

"That they could have come from China?"

"Across five thousand miles of ocean? In a junk?"

Brad's voice had its impatient, patronizing tone. Of course, it was ridiculous, when one thought about it. Brad went on: "It's true the Chinese junk was aerodynamically one of the most efficient sailing vessels ever built. In our world they were voyaging to India in the fourth century, to Africa in the Middle

Ages. But to travel five thousand miles out of sight of land!"

"Okay, okay."

A patter of running feet put an end to conversation. There was a bustle of activity, voices calling in a strange language. Simon crouched lower. He heard the flap of sail, the rattle of an anchor being weighed. He felt alarm at that. If they were setting sail, it knocked the notion of a short swim to shore on the head. But even if they knew in which direction shore was, they couldn't dive overboard at the moment without being spotted. He tried to console himself with the thought that the junk would probably stick close to the coast, anyway—perhaps put in at some point before their final destination, wherever that might be.

After a time, the activity died away, leaving the ordinary sounds of wind and waves and creaking timbers. Simon's head was thumping still; he felt tired, and a bit sick. He dozed and, coming awake, was aware of an area in which the absolute dark was lightening slightly. Dawn. But the odd thing was that the lighter patch wasn't on either port or starboard beam, but directly astern. He pointed that out to Brad.

"Yes, I'd noticed. We may be rounding a headland."

Simon began to be able to see his surroundings more clearly. The junk was bigger than the Roman ship in which they had crossed the Atlantic. There were five masts, each carrying a square lugsail. The sails consisted of a series of panels, stiffened by bamboo battens. According to Brad, these functioned like Venetian blinds. The release of a halyard allowed them to fold on top of one another: a quick way of shortening sail. The mast was unsupported by stays or shrouds. At the stern, there was a high section, like the castle in early Western sailing ships.

The growing light revealed something else—unbroken ocean on all sides. Simon remarked uneasily: "Some headland."

There was a pause before Brad said: "Maybe we'd better get below for the time being. We're a bit conspicuous on deck."

"Down among the zombies?"

"There must be other holds."

Simon was happy to leave Brad in charge of the exploration; he still felt woozy. They found another hatch, and Brad went down while Simon squatted at the top. Brad came back up with an uneasy baffled look on his face.

"It's occupied. And also by deep sleepers."

"More Indians?"

"No. Chinese."

"But . . ."

"It's not so crowded, and they're not lying on bare boards. They've got mats and pillows." He shook his head. "I don't get it."

"Sun's almost up."

"I know. Come on."

They found refuge eventually in a hold packed with sacks and boxes. When they had settled themselves, Simon said: "How far north do you think their home port might be?" Brad did not answer. "Or south?"

Brad said: "Maybe I got it wrong."

"I don't believe it! You got something wrong—*and* you're admitting?"

Brad was preoccupied.

"Time and distance are the problem. You couldn't store enough food and fresh water for the crew of a vessel this big on a voyage lasting that long. And if you pick up a human cargo on the way, it makes it even more impossible. But if the human cargo can sleep through the trip—and you can put the majority of your crew to sleep as well . . . Most of the time you could get by with a handful of men. In emergencies, presumably you could wake them up and send them back to sleep afterwards. It might work. Nothing else fits the facts."

"Are you saying they put the Indians—and a lot of their own men—into some kind of hibernation? How?"

"I don't know. But in our own world there were mystics who claimed they could control metabolism. Even in the West—the *Guinness Book of World Records* included a man who survived ten feet underground for more than a hundred days."

Simon thought about it. "So you think we might be heading for China, after all?"

"Could be."

He thought about that, too. "It's a long swim back already. And it would be a long time to go undetected as stowaways. How many Chinese were there in that hold?"

"A lot. Over fifty."

"And how many awake, crewing, would you say?"

"Once a course was set, two or three should be able to manage."

"Two or three," Simon said, "against two of us. And they don't know we're awake."

Brad nodded. "It's something to think about. But we'd better wait for dark."

It was a long day. They dozed much of the time. At one point, Simon woke with another raging thirst but dared not risk going up on deck to the water tank. When at last the hatch's square of light faded with dusk, he asked Brad: "What's the plan of action?"

"We'll need to reconnoitre—find out how many there are, and where. Then pick them off."

Imminence made the idea less attractive. Simon said: "We might be able to find a dinghy and get away."

"We might. I'd think it was easier to jump the Chinese than launch a dinghy without being spotted. Also, we've been sailing over twelve hours, and we're probably in the Kuroshio current, which does better than two knots across the Pacific. Add on wind speed from five large sails, and that makes quite a distance to row back."

"I suppose you're right. Shall we press on?"

They made a cautious exploration of the deck. Lights showed in the elevated stern section, but they checked the forward deck carefully before heading there. At a suitable observation spot, they settled down to watch comings and goings. One lamp revealed a galley on the lower level, and someone preparing food. Simon whispered: "I make it three— two above and one below."

"Check."

"The one in the galley's on his own. If we got close, we could make some sort of noise to attract his attention and jump him when he came out."

"We could attract the attention of his buddies, too."

Cooking smells wafted to them. It didn't smell a lot like the Chinese food Simon remembered, but it was tantalizing. He could hear the waves slapping against the junk's sides, the hiss of wind in the sails. Then another sound: the small boom of a gong.

"Dinner is served," Brad said. "Which I guess means the other two have to come below. Let's move."

· · ·

The upper stern deck had cabins fronted by a gangway which ran the width of the junk. There was just one companionway, on the port beam. They stationed themselves on either side, in the shadows.

If they came down together, it could be tricky, Simon thought, clutching the billet of wood which was his weapon. But only one pair of footsteps sounded on the gangway overhead, and descended the ladder. As the figure came level, he moved out quickly and swung. There was a realization, both satisfying and sickening, of the blow solidly connecting with flesh, followed by a grunt of exhaled breath.

The man collapsed. Brad ran his hands over him and found a dagger. They pulled him into the shadows as they heard more footsteps. The sick feeling had gone, and Simon felt on top of the world. He counted the descending steps: eleven, twelve . . . Leaping, he swung again, and heard a squawk of anger.

This one staggered, but recovered. Brad launched himself at him from the other side, and they struggled. In the lamplight that spilled from the galley, Simon could see two writhing pairs of legs. He got hold of a leg wearing long baggy trousers and pulled violently. The second Chinese hit the deck with a heavy thump. Brad gathered a dagger from him, too, and handed it to Simon as the cook came out. He obviously didn't suspect anything: he wasn't even carrying a kitchen knife. Seeing the daggers in their hands, he backed away, muttering.

"So far, so good," Simon said happily.

"Don't say that," Brad warned. "Can you bring up one of those coils of rope?"

Simon tied up the two they had ambushed. The first was flat out, the second conscious but not offering opposition. The cook stood by the open galley door.

"Him, too?"

Brad said: "I thought we might talk him into serving supper first."

Simon waggled the dagger, and the cook backed into the galley. On the stove there was a large dish of rice and several smaller dishes. Another gesture with the dagger got the right results. The cook ladled food into bowls and handed them to them.

They ate hungrily, cramming food in with their fingers. There were chopsticks on the table, but Simon didn't think this was the time to start using them. He emptied his bowl and was about to hand it back for a refill when he saw the cook looking past them, towards the open door. Not that old trick, he thought, but his own eyes followed automatically. Another Chinese stood there, holding a stick.

Brad had seen him, too. "Looks like we missed one."

"But only one."

Brad put his bowl down. "I thought it was going too well."

"When I give the signal," Simon said, "we go for him."

"I don't think so."

"When you give the signal, then. What are we waiting for?"

The Chinese raised the stick and said something which sounded like an order.

"I think he wants us to drop the daggers," Brad said.

"Are you saying we should?" Simon stared at him incredulously. "Give in to one man, with a stick?"

"It's not a stick," Brad said.

He reached out and took the dagger from Simon and tossed it, along with his own, to the floor.

"It's a gun."

3

SIMON AWOKE CRAMPED AND STIFF. HE tried to turn over and found that although the upper part of his body responded, something was holding his feet. He took in noises: creaking timbers, sounds of wind and sea, a nearer clanking sound. The clanking began when he tried to move and stopped when he did.

Brad said: "You awake, Si?"

He reached down and touched the chains which hobbled his ankles, and remembered the previous night.

"I'm awake."

Early morning light through a square porthole showed him his surroundings. It was a cabin about six feet by twelve, bare except for the heap of charcoal which took up half the floor area and reached almost to the deck above. Fuel for the galley, presumably.

Brad said: "The door's bolted on the other side. Not that we'd be likely to get far with these leg irons."

Simon examined his ankles. The fetters were steel, of better quality than he had seen this side of the fireball. One was clamped round each ankle, and a very short chain connected them. He now remembered one of the Chinese snapping them shut and locking them with an impressive-looking key.

He asked: "*Where* did that other one come from? I thought we'd checked out."

"He must have been lying low in one of the cabins."

"And that gun . . . I know the Chinese invented gunpowder, but I thought they only used it for fireworks."

"No. The Chinese armies that fought Genghiz Khan in the thirteenth century had quite advanced weapons—grenades, bombs, rocket-powered arrows, even flamethrowers. And what they called the fire-spurting lance. In other words, guns."

Simon was not too interested in Genghiz Khan. "What happens now?"

"Well, they could have chopped us on the spot and tossed us overboard. I think they may be curious about us."

"Would you say that's good?"

"Better than the ocean."

"I suppose so," Simon said. "You know what? I'm hungry again. Very hungry."

"Too bad," Brad said. "That's the trouble with Chinese food."

Day was well advanced when the cabin door was unbolted and thrown open. A Chinese with a dagger gestured towards Brad. Simon got up, too, but was waved back.

Brad said: "Looks like I have the call for first breakfast."

"Don't eat all the ham and eggs."

"I don't guarantee that. But I'll save you a coffee."

The door was slammed and bolted behind him,

and footsteps shuffled away. Simon's wisecracking mood was replaced by an emptiness unrelated to hunger. He was fettered, on a junk in the middle of the Pacific Ocean, at the mercy of a bunch of Chinese about whom he knew nothing except that they were engaged in the slave trade. Even Brad's notion that they had been spared death because their captors were curious took on a less cheering aspect as he considered it. Curiosity could involve a determination to find things out, by any necessary means. He recalled tales of Chinese torture. Comic book stuff, he told himself—but what was a situation in which you were chained and on a Chinese junk *except* comic book stuff?

It was a long time before the cabin door opened again. The same Chinese indicated he should come out, and then pushed him in the direction he was to go. He had to climb stairs to the upper deck—not easy in leg irons. When he faltered, the Chinese pricked him sharply with the dagger.

He was taken to a cabin in the middle of the upper gangway. An announcement was made at the door, in respectful tones, and he was pushed inside.

It was a different world. There were paintings

and decorated silks on the walls, patterned rugs on the floor, silk-shaded hanging lamps in the corners of the room. A sofa bed was heaped with cushions, and at the far end a Chinese sat cross-legged on a luxurious divan, smoking an odd-looking pipe. It was the man with the gun. He had a long face and drooping moustache, and wore a crimson robe. When he lifted his hand to dismiss the guard, Simon noticed manicured fingernails.

As the door closed, the man spoke a few words, in a calm quiet voice. Getting no response, he spoke again. This time, though still not understanding it, Simon recognized the language as something like Chumash, the Indians' tongue.

The Chinese beckoned Simon to approach. He hobbled across the cabin, and another gesture directed him to kneel. Standing in front of him, the Chinese produced a gleaming bronze disk, attached to a black silk cord, from a pocket in his robe. A flick of his fingers set the disk spinning.

Simon looked at it and then looked away. A perfumed hand pulled his head back. The disk still spun. He looked through and past it, visualizing other scenes: a Saturday afternoon's cricket and the sun bursting through after rain, his dog Tarka doing her begging act for chocolate, a winter evening and the smell of roasted chestnuts . . .

Abruptly the disk's spinning was halted. The Chinese put it away and tugged a silken rope, sounding a bell somewhere outside. The guard returned and prodded Simon to the door. He was pushed down the gangway to a narrow deck section which ran alongside the stern castle, and further aft to a small quarterdeck where the anchor lay with its coiled chain in a shallow well.

Simon was close by the bulwark rail, beyond which the swell of water stretched to a hazy horizon. He suddenly wondered about Brad, aware that it would take only a quick heave from the guard behind him to send unwanted goods over into the ocean's depths. Had that happened to Brad? He didn't have much chance, fettered and facing an armed opponent, but it would be better to go out fighting.

He turned to face the guard. The man made a small jab with his dagger, and Simon backed off. If he retreated a bit, then threw himself at him . . . The dagger jerked again, and he retreated another step, and a second. As he tensed muscles, his heel touched something. Glancing round, he saw an open hatch; then lost balance as the guard shoved him. He dropped several feet before he landed, winding himself.

Brad's voice said: "Welcome back."

Groggily, Simon got to his feet.

"I take it you also flunked the test," Brad said.

Simon rubbed his right knee, which had taken the main impact. "What test?"

"Didn't he try hypnosis on you, too?"

"Oh, that. Sure."

"But yours was obviously a shorter session. Maybe my bad reaction put him off. I have a feeling hypnosis could be something they take for granted— it probably ties in with the trance business. It doesn't tie in with what I thought I knew about ancient China, but neither does trancing. I think we really puzzle him."

"So what do you think he's going to do with us?"

"As I say, we puzzle him. We're unusual specimens. Wrong physical appearance, wrong response to hypnosis. If I were him, I'd keep us for study, later."

"Later? Do you mean, in China?"

"Could be. And we're only interesting while we're alive, which means we should get fed and watered. On the other hand, if I have to cross the Pacific on a junk sharing twelve square feet of cabin space with you, I'm going to wind up bored to death or out of my skull."

"I see what you mean," Simon said. "And vice versa."

A few hours later, food and water were lowered in pans on the ends of ropes. The food wasn't exciting—rice with something unidentifiable mixed in—but it satisfied hunger. The next day passed as monotonously. On the third morning, though, a ladder was tossed down, and they climbed it awkwardly into bright sunshine. One of the crew—perhaps the same one—escorted them to the captain's cabin.

This time he wore a green robe, embroidered with little red dragons. He spoke in Chinese. When he got no reply, he pointed at Simon and spoke again.

"I think he wants you to say something," Brad said.

"What?"

"Maybe he just wants to hear what our language sounds like. Say anything."

Simon's mind was a blank. As the Chinese spoke again, more sharply, he suddenly thought of English lessons in school and launched desperately into John of Gaunt's speech from *Richard II*. "This land of such dear souls," he wound up idiotically, "this dear dear land."

"Spoken like a true Brit," Brad said. The Chinese was gazing at them with a look of bafflement. "But I wonder . . ."

He too started reciting. It took Simon a couple of moments to realize he was doing so in Latin, reeling off one of the Christian litanies they had been obliged to learn during their stay in the Bishop's palace. The Chinese listened closely, then raised a hand.

"*Lo ma ni?*" he asked.

"Yes," Brad said, in Latin. "We come as friends and ambassadors from the Roman people. . . ."

The readiness of the lie impressed Simon, but it was wasted. A wave of the hand cut Brad short. The hand pointed to a lamp, and a word was spoken. The Chinese looked at them expectantly.

"He knows about Romans," Brad said, "but he doesn't speak Latin. So we're to learn Chinese."

He repeated the word, and the Chinese nodded approval. He then picked up a small bell, rang it, and said something else.

"Now, did that mean 'the bell' or 'the sound of ringing'?" Brad asked. "Well, we'll find out in time. And we've plenty of that."

During the first session, which lasted over an hour, the Chinese identified himself as Shih Chung-tu. They were called for another lesson the next morning, and thereafter at daily intervals. After a week, Brad was able to conduct a halting conversation. That day they weren't sent back to the hold.

Brad explained: "He thinks it's okay to give us the freedom of the ship. He pointed out we're a long way from land. And, of course, we're hobbled."

"Did you get any idea what he's going to do with us?"

"When we get to China? Well, we intrigue him. By not being susceptible to hypnosis, for one thing, and for another being Roman but at the wrong edge of the Chinese world. That seems to have surprised him as much as finding a pagoda in California did us. I think he feels a bit like someone on a horse-rustling expedition who picks up a couple of zebras. Or giraffes, more likely."

"So what do you think his plans might be for his giraffes?"

Brad nodded. "Lots of possibilities. Put them on public show. Hand them over to a zoologist for a little scientific investigation. Keep them for private display, the way English ladies kept blackamoors in the eighteenth century. Sell them, maybe. If we're potentially of value, it's better, from our point of view, than just being nuisances."

"Did he ask how we came to be where he found us?"

"Yes. I pretended I didn't understand that bit."

"I don't suppose it would do any harm to say we fled across the great water after the rebellion against the Roman emperor, and then kept on travelling. It's roughly true."

"The sensible giraffe doesn't start explaining its neck."

"Perhaps not." Simon paused. "Do you think the wind's getting up?"

"Yes. And the sky's looking dirty. That was a

shorter session, and he went forward afterwards. He may think it's the moment for calling up extra hands. By the way, I think I've worked out how we came to miss him at the beginning."

"How?"

"If they can apply that trance sleep to one another, they can probably slip into it themselves. As the captain, he wouldn't want to be out for too long, but short spells would break up the monotony and conserve energy. It was our bad luck he set his mental alarm for that particular time." He pointed along the deck. "I was right about the extra hands."

Chung-tu was standing beside the hold containing the bulk of the crew. He produced a small gong and striker from inside his robe. The ringing, twice repeated, was carried to them on the freshening wind. Soon a head appeared from the hatch, followed by others. Within a minute, the deck was boiling with Chinese.

The storm blew up fast and lasted through that day and the following night. The resuscitated crew worked with noisy cheerfulness as the junk rolled before a northeasterly gale. The vessel showed its seaworthiness; although things became uncomfortable, Simon never felt the situation was getting out of hand.

In the middle of the next day, with sea and wind moderating, a large meal was served; and afterwards all but three—a different three, Simon thought, but could not be sure—retired to the hold.

Next morning the Chinese lessons were resumed, and as the days passed their grasp of the language improved. Brad reached the point where he could ask fairly complex questions and understand most of what Chung-tu said in reply.

The technique for putting people into deep trance, he said, had been known for hundreds of years. Apart from its value on long voyages, it had other advantages—in the healing of certain sicknesses, for instance. It was part of the Laws of Bei-Kun—of the lower part. The higher part was sacred, known only to the priests of Bei-Kun.

Brad asked about the Indians. They were highly prized, Chung-tu told them, as personal attendants by the gentry of the Celestial Kingdom. They would not be required to labour in the fields like peasants, but would live lives of comparative ease. It was their high value which justified such an expedition as this, across the greatest of oceans.

But another question from Brad drew what was plainly a rebuke. Simon asked him about it later.

"I goofed," Brad said. "I said I supposed if they were so valuable this would be a very profitable trip. He didn't like that."

"Why not?"

"He said he was a humble servant of the Son of Heaven, concerned only to do the Son of Heaven's will. I was implying he was acting as a merchant, and the Chinese gentry despise merchants."

"But he stands to get something out of it, surely?"

"Of course he does. Honours, land—probably bags of gold, too. It's the sort of arrangement Elizabeth the First had with men like Raleigh. He gives the slaves to the Emperor and gets presents, and the Emperor passes the slaves on to courtiers in the same way. It's not really trade, or you can pretend it isn't."

"How do they know how much to give?"

"By the way the Emperor holds his fan."

Simon looked baffled.

"Not literally. But the Chinese are a subtle lot. He would have a hundred ways of indicating he wasn't satisfied—apart from the simple ones like taking people off his party list. Or calling up the Lord High Executioner."

"Anyway, it doesn't sound too bad a life as far as the Indians are concerned."

"No, but slavery's slavery, whether they tie you with a rope or a golden tassel." Brad frowned. "I wish I could understand the Bei-Kun business."

"Wouldn't he explain?"

"My Chinese isn't up to it. Obviously it's some sort of religion. The ancient Chinese were divided for a long time between Confucianism and Buddhism, with Confucianism finally winning out. Maybe Bei-Kun was a new prophet in this world. But how does it fit with the fireball?"

"I don't know," Simon said. "You worry about it. This giraffe's more concerned with what happens when we get to China."

The tedious days grew into monotonous weeks. Three more times the crew was awakened to deal with bad weather, subsequently returning to hibernation. Simon found himself envying them. For a period of over a week, they had no summons to Chung-tu's cabin: he guessed the captain had grown bored with the lessons and opted for trance.

Then one morning an excited cry from one of the crew brought the other two to the port bow. Brad and Simon hobbled after them to find them hanging over the rail. The sea was calm to a misty horizon, but there was something just discernible: a promontory of land.

"China?" Simon asked.

"More likely one of the islands between Japan and Formosa."

The spit of land eventually fell away to stern, and they sailed on into broad empty waters. But a few days later, after the daily fix of position had been made, Chung-tu sounded his gong, and the rest of the crew came hurrying up on deck.

Soon they were swarming the length and breadth of the ship, scrubbing and cleaning, polishing and painting. Some swung dizzily from ropes attached to the tops of the masts, painting the sails' bamboo battens gold. When they had finished, the junk looked like a different vessel. Chung-tu made a leisurely inspection and then took his gong to the hold where the Indians lay.

Sounds from within indicated a return to consciousness. Normal at first, they were soon punctuated by cries of grief and misery. Then, on orders from Chung-tu, figures started to appear on deck. They moved slowly and clumsily, like people emerging from a drugged sleep. Some were being carried by others. Sleeping still, Simon thought, until the unmistakable smell of corruption told him this was not sleep, but death.

On a further command, the bearers took their dead companions to the side of the junk and slid them into the sea. There was no ceremony. Simon remembered the funeral of a young Indian who had been killed on a hunting expedition, which had gone on for hours with chanting and sobbing, and the shamans dancing.

"I've counted fifteen so far," Simon said, as a brave who had sat close by him at the feast was dropped overboard. "What do you think went wrong?"

"Hibernation must be very close to death. I suppose some were physically weaker or more frightened, or something. I don't know. But it puts things in a different perspective, doesn't it? It *seemed* reasonably civilized, as slaving goes. Not like our African slave ships with their holds crammed with poor suffering wretches. It's just as ruthless, though. Look at Chung-tu; there's no surprise on his face. The number of deaths is probably average for a voyage like this."

The Indians were still coming up. Two of them carried between them a female corpse. Night Eagle and Stone Blade were the bearers: the body was that of Little Green Bird.

"Slavery's slavery," Brad said. "And death is death. There's no way of prettying them up."

4

THE HARBOUR WAS IMPRESSIVE; BUSIER and more crowded than any Simon had seen, though the vessels were small by *QE2* standards. Their junk was among the largest. But the really amazing thing was that, while most were sailing ships, there were paddleboats as well; and the paddleboats carried tall thin chimneys puffing black smoke.

"So they have steam power," Brad said. "I suppose it's not all that improbable when you think about it. The Chinese were skilled metallurgists when King Alfred was burning the cakes. Marco Polo made a comment on the amount of black stone there was lying around."

"Coal?"

Brad nodded. "It's not unreasonable that a Chinese Watt could have come up with steam propulsion."

"So why is this a sailing junk—and most of the other ships, for that matter?"

"Coal's a bulky fuel, too bulky for long voyages unless you make the leap in scale to really big carriers—and that depended on the massive increase in trading that came in with capitalism. And remember, the Chinese despised traders. I'd guess the skippers of those paddle steamers rank way below Chung-tu socially."

It was a grey calm morning, and the junk steered a slow course through the assembly of craft. While the Indians squatted apathetically in a well deck aft of the main mast, the Chinese seamen were everywhere, chattering excitedly.

Brad was staring with fascination at the approaching shore. Behind and between the wharves, Simon saw the roofs of a large town, a city more likely. Further back, misty hills merged with the drab sky.

Brad asked sharply: "Did you see that?"

"What?"

"On that waterfront street—no, it's gone."

"What was it?"

"A wagon."

"I can see dozens of them."

"A *steam* wagon," Brad said. "But again, why not?"

Chung-tu did not appear until they were tying up. He wore a tunic of creamy stiff brocade with jade buttons, over green silk trousers and pearl-studded pointed shoes, and carried an enamelled fly whisk. He also had a tall green silk hat, embroidered with pearls. He looked truly comic, but Simon decided against laughing.

Chung-tu took up a position on the port side and stayed there while a gangplank was laid and secured. Simon expected him to go ashore, but he remained where he was. Minutes passed.

Brad was twitching. "What's this about?"

"I don't know. Waiting for Customs?"

Gulls had followed them most of the morning and were now screaming round the stern. They were smaller than the ones Simon remembered, with chocolate heads on top of white blue-winged bodies, but they made at least as much noise as herring gulls. He was watching them when Brad nudged him.

A double line of soldiers had appeared on the wharf. They wore helmets and breastplates, and escorted a litter borne by half a dozen loin-clothed American Indians, which was set down near the foot of the gangplank. The litter's curtains were parted, and the officer in charge helped someone out and deferentially escorted him on board the junk.

The newcomer was dressed even more magnificently than Chung-tu. His crimson silk robe was crusted with gold, and a high peaked hat carried an ornate gold and silver superstructure. He was tall and portly. Chung-tu greeted him with a very low bow, then led him to the spot where his human cargo squatted forlornly.

The crimson-robed man moved slowly among the Indians, appraising them. He stared into a face here, pinched an arm there. After the inspection, he turned to Chung-tu and spoke briefly; his voice sounded approving. The officer barked a command, and two soldiers came on board and shepherded the Indians down the gangplank and away along the wharf.

The Indians outnumbered their guards forty or fifty to one. If they scattered and ran, some would be bound to get clear. Were they still hypnotized, Simon wondered? But where, anyway, could they run to, in a land where their physical appearance all too plainly branded them as foreigners? It reminded him, depressingly, that the same applied to Brad and himself.

Chung-tu gestured respectfully in the direction of his cabin. The big man started to move that way, then stopped. His glance had taken in Simon and Brad. He asked a question and, when Chung-tu answered, strode to where they stood.

At close quarters, his dress and accoutrements were even more obviously those of a very important man. Simon was wondering just how important when Chung-tu screamed an order: "Make obeisance!"

He wasted no time in obeying, but Chung-tu was not satisfied.

"Lower! Prostrate your miserable bodies before His Supreme Excellency, the Lord Yuan Chu, Grand Chancellor to the ineffable and almighty Son of Heaven!"

. . .

The imperial palace was a conglomeration of buildings of varying shapes and sizes, interspersed with
courts and gardens and walkways hung with flower-
ing plants. It covered hundreds of acres, and a high
stone wall separated it from the teeming city beyond.
They were housed in one of the smaller outlying
buildings, in the care of an old woman who chattered
volubly in an unintelligible dialect.

No one came near them for the remainder of the
first day; nor on the following morning. Brad said:
"I suppose Madam Butterfly"—he nodded towards
the old lady—"would raise an alarm if we pushed
off. Unless we tied her up and gagged her."

"I imagine she'd scream blue murder if we tried,
and there are plenty of people within earshot."

"Or we could get away at night."

"There's a wall, and a guard on the gate."

"The wall's climbable. No more than ten feet,
and not sheer."

"That would only get us into the city. We'd be
spotted straight away as foreigners."

"At night all cats are grey. We could be clear
before morning."

"We'd still be whites, in a country of yellows."

"We've been whites in a country of reds."

"I've got a feeling the Chinese might be more curious than the Indians were. And better organized."

"True," Brad said. He looked about him. Their room was about twelve feet square, with walls and ceiling of bamboo and thick paper decorated with flowers. Two of the walls had windows, unglazed but fitted with roller blinds. The front door was open to a view of ornamental shrubs, and a smaller bead-curtained doorway at the back gave access to the room where the old lady lived, and made the tea which she brought them, along with little sweet cakes, at frequent intervals.

"And so far it's not so bad, is it? Not quite like a suite in the Waldorf Astoria, but not a prison cell, either."

That afternoon the Lord Yuan Chu honoured them with his presence. He brought with him a thin-faced man with a shaven head who wore a blue robe and carried a thin black stick, a sort of wand. The robe was of rough cotton, his sandals of simple leather. After they had made obeisance, Yuan Chu introduced him to them as Bei Tsu, a priest of Bei-Kun. He told them to obey the priest in all things, and got back into his litter.

What followed was a variation, or variations, on the procedure Chung-tu had tried unsuccessfully on the junk. The priest had a small leather satchel and from it produced a disk which he held before them and spun, chanting in a soporific voice as he did so. When this had no effect, he switched to making complicated passes with his hands. That having failed, too, he called Madam Butterfly to pull down the blinds.

In a low voice, Brad said: "I wonder if we should try going along with it—pretend we're hypnotized?"

"I think he'd know the difference."

"I guess you're right. So, what next?"

Madam Butterfly scuttled from the darkened room, and Bei Tsu brought out a small lamp, which he lit and set on the floor. Over it he placed a milky white translucent hemisphere. They squatted round it, and the chanting began again.

It went on for a long time, and at one point Simon wondered if it might be having an effect: the surrounding darkness, the flickering light, and the monotonous chanting combined to make him drowsy. But realizing that, he fought against it. He thought discomfort might help, and braced his feet hard against the floor. Soon after, Bei Tsu dowsed the lamp and called Madam Butterfly to pull up the blinds.

The session was not over, though. The priest turned from attempted hypnosis to lecturing. He was telling them about the Laws of Bei-Kun, and a couple of times paused to ask them if they understood. Simon nodded, though his feeling was he wouldn't have understood it even in English.

At the end, the priest clapped his hands, and Madam Butterfly brought in tea and cakes. Taking refreshment with them, Bei Tsu asked polite questions about the land of the Lomani, which Brad answered. He nodded in acceptance.

"It has been said that the Lomani are people of earth, not of wind or fire. They cultivate second mind. It is not surprising you cannot enter into the way of peace."

When he had gone, Simon asked: "How much of that spiel did you get? Anything? First mind . . . second mind—what was he on about?"

"I'm not sure. As far as I can make out, the basic

notion is that we have two minds, not one. Second mind is our ordinary consciousness—what we do our thinking with. First mind is something deeper, more fundamental. Second mind works through the brain, first mind doesn't."

"So what does it work through?" Brad shrugged. "And what are the laws that are so important?"

"The law of suggestion seems to be the big one. First mind is supposed to be totally governed by suggestion. It does what it's told—by second mind chiefly, but also by other people's second minds. And according to Bei Tsu, by devils and by the divine spirit. Being hypnotized puts you into the way of peace, where first mind can function freely."

"And that means doing as it's told by whoever's on the other end of the hypnotizing. Great deal. Look where it got the Indians."

"I don't see the point of it myself, but he claims there are advantages. Anyway, he wasn't too surprised it didn't work with us. People of earth, the Lomani."

"That sounded like a nasty crack."

"I don't think it was meant to be. The Chinese regard all foreigners as beneath contempt, but they don't mean it unkindly. I wonder what comes next, now we've been tried and found wanting a second time."

What came next was a summons to the imperial palace. The Lord Chancellor's bodyguard escorted them through a bewildering succession of courts and colonnades. At one point, they passed between bronze gates, guarded by tall soldiers, into what was obviously the citadel. On the far side, the gardens looked as immaculate as if they had been trimmed with nail scissors but were full of exotic plants, and pools dense with gross golden fish. Eventually, through an open bronze door decorated with a tangled riot of dragons in high relief, they entered a high-ceilinged room, more than a dozen yards across and twice that in length. The walls were deep crimson, inset with ivory panels carved to give an impression of a forest of moonlit trees. People in gaudy dress stood talking; one, who beckoned them imperiously to him, was the Lord Yuan Chu.

They followed him over a deep-pile carpet in concentric arcs of yellow, successively deeper in shade. At the innermost arc, the Lord Chancellor dropped to his knees and touched the floor with his forehead, and Brad and Simon followed suit. There was a dais just ahead, with a golden throne. Simon guessed they were in the presence of the Son of Heaven himself, the Emperor.

On the throne sat a figure wearing a tunic of bright yellow silk and a golden headdress trimmed with large pearls. Daring at last to look at him directly, Simon was amazed. He was expecting someone venerable, and probably very old; what he saw was a frail-looking boy of about fourteen.

The interview was brief. They were introduced by the Lord Chancellor, who thanked the Celestial One on their behalf for his condescension in admitting them to his sacred presence. Then, after the Emperor had uttered a few words of acknowledgement in a thin colourless voice, all three retired, walking awkwardly backwards. The escort returned them to their hut, and it seemed that was that.

The following morning, though, the Lord Chancellor visited them again. He announced that a great honour, unprecedented for barbarians, had befallen them. The Son of Heaven had decreed that they were to join his household: they would take up residence in the Crimson Palace right away.

He studied them with a cold eye.

"It is not possible for you to show sufficient gratitude for this favour, Lomani. But at least you will remember your unworthiness of it. You will understand that to offend the Celestial One in the smallest item merits flogging; in any other than the smallest, death. Nor can you expect such a death to be easy."

He paused. "And remember, also, that the Lord Yuan Chu, the humble servant of the Son of Heaven, has a thousand eyes which watch you always."

The reality, after this menacing introduction, proved surprisingly pleasant. Rigid protocol governed the actual throne room, but outside it life was simpler. Four heavily armed Indian guards attended the Emperor constantly, but they were silent and unobtrusive, and one soon came to ignore their presence.

There was certainly nothing frightening about the boy emperor, Cho-tsing. They had to greet him with the ritual of obeisance, but after that informality was the order of the day. He proved, in fact, to be an unassuming, almost diffident character.

This emerged clearly when it came to playing games. There was, for instance, a ball game played in something like a squash court, in which you hit the ball with a bat strapped to the lower arm. He introduced them to this but was not himself very good at it. He demonstrated it playing against one of the guards, and it was obvious at once that the guard was playing for him to win. Simon, when the Emperor asked him to take the guard's place, started on the same tack, but after a few minutes, in the excitement of the game, found himself playing naturally, which meant outplaying the Son of Heaven. A warning call from Brad, who was a spectator, brought him up short, and he resumed his previous tactic. But the Emperor stopped the game and, shaking his head in a very unimperial way, told him to play his best.

He had been, as far as they could tell, totally deprived of companions of his own age—indeed, of any real companions—and it was surprising that, despite this, he could adapt so well to the concept of give and take. He seemed quite content to accept being beaten by Simon and subsequently by Brad. They were both naturally better than he was, and after a time, in fact, on the Emperor's suggestion, they played more often against one another while he watched and cheerfully applauded.

The situation was somewhat different with chess, which they played on a gold and silver squared board, with pieces carved from light and dark jade. There Simon was weakest, Brad and Cho-tsing more of an equal match. But there, too, after Brad had taken the measure of the Emperor's play, he began to win consistently and again without any sign of resentment from his high-born opponent.

The chess games tended to be drawn out, and during them Simon amused himself slamming a ball round the court, or teasing and being teased by the palace monkeys. These wore jewelled leather jackets, were noisy and lively, and could be vicious. Though not, Simon noticed, with Cho-tsing, who was gentle with them and to whom they were unfailingly gentle in return. He was plainly fond of them, and they of him—Simon wondered if anyone else here was.

It was not that he was short of company. Apart from the Lord Chancellor, a frequent visitor, there were the ladies of the court who lived in adjoining palaces. His mother, also quiet and gentle, was a small plump woman, the Lady Cho Pi. He also had dozens of aunts and female cousins, chattering and giggling behind their fans. And after they had been in the palace a few days, they were summoned to the presence of the Lady Lu T'Sa, the Dowager Empress.

Her palace was almost as grand as the Emperor's, lavishly decorated in ivory and jade and silver. She perched on an ebony and ivory throne, a tiny figure swathed in a cloak of green brocade studded with a swarm of silver dragonflies, wearing a high green headdress with ropes of amber and garnet beads. Her face was small and wrinkled—they guessed she was Cho-tsing's grandmother, or possibly his great-grandmother. After she had questioned them in a thin rasping voice, she called Cho-tsing to private audience, and he was a long time absent.

Brad said: "Did you see the way she and Yuan Chu looked at one another? No love lost there. Rivals, I'd guess, and in quite a serious way."

"Rivals?"

"The one person who doesn't have power here is Cho-tsing. He's been Emperor since he was a child, but the Lady Lu T'Sa's been in charge of things. She means to keep it like that, but I've a notion Yuan Chu may have other ideas. She mistrusts him, and therefore mistrusts us, since he's introduced us to the palace. Those questions, wanting to know exactly which part of the Western empire we came from . . . and that remark at the end—that she'd met other Lomani in her long life, but we were different . . ."

"If she does mistrust us, does it mean we could be in trouble?"

"I don't think right now, but it bears watching."

Simon thought about it. "Do you think Yuan Chu did have some special reason for bringing us into the palace? And if so, what?"

"Probably yes to the first. On the second, I don't know. It may be connected with our not being hypnotizable, but it could also be that he thought he might be able to control Cho-tsing through us, if we became his friends. And that he was ripe for a change from all these women around him."

"There are a lot of women," Simon added, as a random thought. "And they all walk funny."

"It's their feet."

"Is it?" Simon frowned. "You can't *see* their feet, with those dresses sweeping the floor."

"You aren't supposed to—feet are the big taboo. But if you could see them you'd understand about the walk. It's called the lily walk and comes from having their feet tightly bound when they're small. They turn into little hooves."

"I've seen Madam Butterfly's feet. They're normal—a bit big, actually."

"It doesn't apply to the lower classes. A serving woman, like a man, needs feet she can use. A noble lady doesn't need to do anything, or even walk far—there's always someone to carry her. Did you notice the long fingernails, too? In our world, some Chinese ladies had nails so long they couldn't do *anything*, even feed themselves."

"But why? To prove they were ladies?"

"And because the men found it attractive."

"Attractive?" Simon pulled a face.

"It's all relative. Beauty's an illusion, isn't it?"

There was a banquet that evening, at which the Emperor sat surrounded by the ladies of the court. The only male near was the Lord Chancellor, seated at his left hand. The Lady Lu T'Sa was on his right. Simon and Brad were at the far end of the long table, which suited Simon: whatever might be going on between the Lord Chancellor and the Dowager

Empress, he was happy to be away from the scene of the action.

The food was good, though Simon still found chopsticks difficult, and the succession of tiny cups of tea became boring. He guessed there would be entertainment later and wondered what kind— dancers, jugglers, musicians? Musicians did appear and took up positions near the head of the table, but what followed was more surprising. Serving girls went round extinguishing the lamps, leaving just two burning on bronze pillars in the centre of the room. The ladies' chatter subsided into an expectant silence; and into the remaining pool of light came neither dancers nor jugglers, but the priest, Bei Tsu.

Solemnly he intoned prayers to the Great Spirit, first of all first minds. He made rapid complicated twirling motions with his wand. Then he put out the remaining lamps.

In total darkness, the musicians struck up jangling music: there were strings and some wind instrument playing wailing half-tones, irregularly punctuated by a drum. After some time, to Simon's relief, it ceased, leaving a silence that seemed deeper and more absolute than before. He wondered what came next, and went on wondering as moments ticked into minutes. Suddenly there was a scratch of flint on metal, a spark, the glow of a taper. The priest relit the lamps. Turning back to face the top of the banqueting table, he said: "The manifestations of first mind are thwarted by hostile thoughts. This accords with the law of suggestion, as pronounced by the sage, Bei-Kun."

The serving girls were relighting the other lamps. The priest turned to the other end of the table and fixed his eyes accusingly on Brad and Simon.

"The spirits of wind and fire turn away from the earthbound ones and absent themselves."

A further silence followed. Simon wasn't sure whether to feel embarrassed or apprehensive: since he had no idea what he might have done wrong, he could think of no way of putting it right. He glanced along the table. Yuan Chu was impassive, but Cho-tsing looked worried. It was the Dowager Empress, though, who spoke.

"The earthbound ones will leave the room," the Lady Lu T'Sa said. "Begone, Lomani!"

• • •

Brad was as baffled as Simon by what had happened. They agreed the only thing they could do was wait and see what came next. In the morning, as usual, they were summoned into the presence of the Son of Heaven.

Cho-tsing behaved as though the incident hadn't occurred. They accompanied him to his favourite pool, where Brad had been teaching him the crawl stroke. It was made of pink and white marble with a green jade rim, set in a small forest of miniature trees and starlike flowers. When they were lying in the sun after swimming, Brad asked about the previous evening: in what way had they offended?

Cho-tsing smiled, and shook his head.

"You do not understand the Laws of Bei-Kun, B'lad."

"So explain them."

"It is too difficult, I think." He paused. "Tell me about your land, the country of the Lomani."

"Tell you what?"

"Everything."

Brad shook his head, in turn. "There's too much."

"That is the problem. Our beginnings lie very far

apart and cannot be brought together. It is enough that you have come here, over many thousands of leagues. Of that I am glad."

The words were spoken quietly, but with conviction. It was a remark that Simon, accustomed to the unsentimental and unemotional nature of his association with Brad, would have expected to find embarrassing, but he did not. He felt instead a wave of affection for this thin boy, ruler—so-called—of the farflung empire of the East. And felt pity also. Being emperor meant, inevitably, being used by others. He had nothing, including the companionship he had found with them, which was not at risk.

They were again at the pool, three days later, when they were visited by the priest. They had tired of swimming and were amusing themselves in the shallower part, trying to catch the fish which darted round their feet. Bei Tsu called them, and they left the pool reluctantly. The visit was probably, Simon thought, aimed at Brad and him—probably another lecture on the Laws of Bei-Kun was in prospect.

He was right in the first part of the surmise, wrong in the second. Bei Tsu informed them that a decision had been taken. The Lomani were to go to the Bonzery of Grace, where they would receive instruction from the priests of Bei-Kun.

"No," Cho-tsing said. "I do not wish this."

He looked very young, with a yellow drying robe over his narrow shoulders, twisting his hands together.

"It is necessary."

"But at least not yet!"

"They are to go today, Celestial One."

"I will speak with the Lord Chancellor."

Bei Tsu looked at him impassively.

"It is the Lady Lu T'Sa's command."

Cho-tsing's shoulders drooped, and he said no more.

5

THE CANAL STARTED NOT FAR FROM THE imperial city of Li Nan and ran northwest across the broad Kiangsu plain. Green paddy fields, dotted with labouring coolies of both sexes, stretched away on either side. It was a very wide canal: their barge, which was itself large, fitted with a lugsail and also manned by oarsmen, ten to a side, rocked in the wake of a passing steam-driven freight barge at least forty yards long.

Simon said: "I still don't understand why she was so determined to get us away. Just because Bei Tsu thought we mucked up the stunts at the banquet?"

"I doubt it. She wanted us away from the Son of Heaven, more likely."

"Why? She didn't think we were a danger to him, surely?"

"She may have thought we might give him ideas."

"About what?"

"I don't know," Brad said. "Yes, I do. About anything. As it is, he's surrounded by guards and eunuchs and aunts—no one near his own age. It all helps keep him under control, and keeping the Son of Heaven under control is the name of the game."

The day was overcast, grey but not cold. The oarsmen were sweating. Simon said: "She didn't need to send us to the Bonzery of Grace. She could have had us killed. I'd think she's capable of it."

"Very capable," Brad agreed. "But she knew he liked us. It could have been risking trouble, even with someone as docile as Cho-tsing. Whereas he couldn't object to something done in the name of Bei-Kun. Mind you, out of sight is out of mind."

Simon looked alarmed. "You don't think? . . ."

"No." Brad nodded towards one of the guards who were accompanying them, along with Bei Tsu. "They wouldn't have bothered putting us on board—we could have been killed just outside the city wall. We're heading for the bonzery, all right."

"And religious instruction? That doesn't exactly turn me on."

"Better than death by torture for being bad influences on the Son of Heaven. It might be interesting in a way. We might even discover what the Laws of Bei-Kun are about."

Simon shook his head. "I can get by without that."

The barge travelled slowly north. Their canal met and crossed the turbulent waters of the Yangtse and debouched eventually into the Yellow River. Their course was westwards now, and on a bright morning they left the barge at a village on the river's north bank and struck inland. Brad and Simon and the priest were supplied with mules; the guards travelled on foot. The road was reasonably good at first, with a fair amount of horse and ox traffic; but gradually they advanced into the foothills of a mountain range, and the road dwindled into a track. There were fewer travellers, then none.

They spent a chilly night by the side of the trail

and in the morning were surrounded by mist which showed no signs of lifting. After breakfasting on cold rice and dried fish, they resumed their journey on a path which climbed steadily higher. It was impossible to see more than a yard or two on either side. Progress was tedious, and Simon found himself nodding off from time to time. In the middle of the day, a pale disk of sun briefly offered glimpses of mountain spurs, twisted trees, the gleam of a tumbling waterfall. They refilled water bottles there and rested the animals.

Afterwards the mist settled down thicker than before. Nor did its occasional thinnings provide any reassuring outlook: one sudden view into a ravine plunging within feet of the track prickled the hairs at the back of Simon's head. It was very quiet. The guards, who had earlier talked cheerfully among themselves, fell silent. The only sounds were footfalls and the padding of the mules, both eerily muffled by the mist.

Simon started wondering about the next night stop. He was not sure whether the mist was deepening or dusk was coming on. The thought of another night in the open was daunting: it would be a lot colder at the height they must have reached by now.

But almost on that instant there was an extraordinary change. A doubtful brightening ahead swiftly turned to gold, and then to full visibility as his mule lurched into the clarity of late afternoon. He saw deep blue sky and the sun's orb seemingly poised on a mountain peak ahead.

The path in front continued to rise, but through cropped grass; white goats grazed among bushes and small trees. Brad came up from behind to bring his mule alongside Simon's.

"There's a sight for sore eyes," he said.

Looking at the sun, Simon said: "I'd almost given up hope of seeing it again."

"No, there." Brad pointed to the left, up beyond the goats and trees.

"Shangri-La, wouldn't you say?"

Simon could remember a holiday he had spent with an aunt in a small dreary north-country town when he was nine or ten. The first couple of days, when rain kept him indoors, had been terribly dull; but at last the weather cleared, and he was able to go for a walk. The nearby countryside was as drab as the town—fields of potatoes and beet—but then he turned a corner in a lane and saw coming towards him, incredibly, a man with an elephant.

His aunt, when he told her, was unimpressed: the farm belonged to a circus family, who sometimes sent animals down there for convalescence. It wasn't remarkable that he had seen an elephant being exercised.

For him, though, it was and remained one of the most astonishing and thrilling encounters of his life. He felt the same way about the building that now confronted him. Behind was the mist through which they had plodded for so many weary hours; ahead, clear and sunlit, lay a mountain landscape whose jagged wildness seemed totally divorced from and alien to human activities. But also there, nestling beneath the mountain peak, was an elaborate and extensive complex of buildings, which must have taken decades, perhaps centuries, to erect.

They were red and white against the grey of rock. On closer view, he could see that the white was granite, the red timber. He marvelled again at its existence here. The granite might have been quarried somewhere nearby, though he saw no evidence of that, but the wood must have been carried all the way up from the plains.

The massive gates were open, revealing a long drive of stone flags flanked by blossoming gardens. He saw irises and peonies, lilies and lupins, and low-lying gold-cupped flowers that looked like over-sized celandines. Except that, obviously, they weren't. Celandines were marsh plants which could not sur-vive at such an altitude.

An archway led to a courtyard, where they parted from the guards. Bei Tsu conducted them to a patio with a pool where fat fish floated in the shade of water lilies. At the far side, two snarling porcelain dogs, oversized Technicolor Pekingese, guarded a doorway. They went through to a hall whose floor and ceiling were black, walls a deep rose-gold, fur-nished only with two low tables on which lamps stood. The hall gave on to a corridor, with more lamps in niches. At the end of it, before a second doorway, Bei Tsu stood to one side, put his hands together, and bowed his head in farewell.

His departing footsteps echoed as they went in. This room was smaller and not so bare. A frieze about a yard in depth ran round the walls, depicting a continuous landscape: mountains and valleys, rivers and lakes and waterfalls, deer-parks and villages succeeded one another. It was a living landscape, with birds and fish and small animals, peasants working, mandarins contemplating nature. The ceiling here was creamy white, and the walls blue above a polished azure floor. Lamps glowed behind blue glass. A smell of something like incense came from enamelled bronze urns set at intervals along the walls. There was furniture: tables and chairs.

"Is this the guest room?" Brad asked. "Those mats over there look as though they're meant for sleeping on."

Simon felt unsettled. "Is it all right to talk?"

"Who's to stop us? Who's here, anyway? They maybe don't need guards on top of a mountain—but no servants? No hellos?"

"Perhaps we're meant to wait here till someone comes."

Brad went over to a table on which there were various bowls and dishes.

"A waiting room, laid for supper?" He examined the display more closely. "Rice, of course, and rice cakes. But this looks like fish in some kind of sauce. And *that* is cold lobster. And look here."

He picked something from a bowl and held it up: an apple.

Simon said: "I suppose it could have been brought up from the valley."

"The apples in Li Nan were still tiny. This is ripe."

"An early variety?"

"*And* we're a couple of hundred miles farther north. And what about this?"

There was a twig attached to the fruit, and the twig had a leaf. Brad plucked and smelled it.

"Fresh."

"So how do you account for it?"

"I wish I knew," Brad said. "It's all crazy. Those flowers blooming outside. . . . None of it makes sense."

Simon had followed him to the table. In the bowls he saw cherries and pomegranates, yellow berries he did not recognize, purple plums. With a feeling of recklessness, he took a plum and bit into it: juice ran down his chin.

"Tastes great," he said.

Brad was staring at the apple. "It just can't be real. There's no way you can have cherries and apples ripe at the same time."

Simon finished eating the plum and tucked the stone away behind the bowl. He felt more hungry rather than less. He took a small bowl and filled it with the food on display. Brad, after some hesitation, followed suit. There were chopsticks and a flask containing wine. They ate and drank, and Simon refilled his empty bowl.

Brad had put his down and was staring round the room with a puzzled, almost angry look.

"It's not some kind of illusion," he said. "You can't eat illusions. So what is it?"

"Does it matter? We didn't eat better even in Cho-tsing's palace."

Suddenly, though, Simon felt a chill of apprehension. It was like being in a fairy story—the vast mansion at the mountain top, no one in evidence, tables laid for a feast. . . . That was the kind of scene, he remembered, which usually ended badly, when the giant returned, or the troll, or the wicked witch.

"There has to be an explanation," Brad said.

He told himself it was a long time since he had

believed in fairy stories; at the same time, he wished Brad would stop fussing about it. He said brusquely: "It can wait till morning. I'm dead beat."

He unrolled one of the mats and lay on it. Something else was odd, he realized; although there was no sign of heating, it did not feel cold. He decided against mentioning that to Brad, in case it brought on another fit of speculation. Anyway, he was very tired. Weariness soon dragged him down into sleep.

In this dream, Simon was once more back in the time before the fireball, resting on a river bank on a drowsy summer's day. The voice crept into the dream. It was low, lulling, scarcely distinguishable from the sound of the breeze in the willows. Gradually it grew closer and louder. He could tell it was a man's voice, though he could not make out what it was saying. He became aware of something else, too—hands on his wrists, gentle but firm, holding him.

He was in some twilight state between sleep and waking. He heard tinkling music, a pattern of notes rising, then falling. The voice began to take on meaning.

"There is nothing to fear. Be at peace. Bid second mind be still. Be at peace. There is nothing to fear. Be at peace, be at peace. . . ."

He had a sense of time having stopped; or perhaps of it being caught up in a loop, with notes and words repeating, forever and ever. He felt he was slipping into something unknown and unknowable, like a rudderless boat drifting downstream. Towards what—an open lock, a weir? Uncertainty became doubt, suspicion, fear. His mind shut tight against the voice.

"Be at peace. There is nothing to fear."

He resisted still, on the edge of panic but refusing to surrender. He had an image of a small animal caught in a trap, wire tightening round it as it struggled. He would not give in. Then somehow the image changed: the small animal was being lifted from its confinement by strong but gentle hands.

"There is nothing to fear. . . ."

And, unaccountably but wonderfully, it was true. Fear went, like a cloud from in front of the sun. The voice was stronger and gave him strength.

"Peace, and the mingling of minds . . . peace, and the mingling of minds . . ."

He was aware of a second voice and realized it was his own, echoing: "Peace, and the mingling of minds . . ."

Then it happened. It was not so much a voice in his mind now as a mind in his mind. No words were spoken, but the message was clearer and surer than speech.

"Friend, you are welcome at the Bonzery of Grace."

Brad's hand on his arm wakened Simon. He asked: "What time is it?"

"Morning, or near enough. It's beginning to get light outside."

"You've been out?"

"Just to look."

"No sign of anyone?"

"No."

The recollection hit him as he got up. He asked Brad: "Did you dream during the night, by any chance?"

"Music," Brad said. "Hands—a girl's voice. Peace, and the mingling of minds."

Simon shook his head. "Not a girl."

Brad shrugged. "I'm telling you my dream."

"And a sort of telepathic welcome at the end?"

"Something like that."

"It must tie up. Dreams don't come in duplicates. What sort of weird stuff goes on here?"

Brad did not answer, which Simon found slightly surprising after his nagging questions the previous evening. He had an odd look—remote but relaxed, happy.

The sound of footsteps came from the corridor, and they both turned towards the door. Now, Simon thought, there might be some explanation.

The man who came in was in his fifties. He wore a simple blue tunic which left his arms and lower legs bare. Except for his face, he looked like a peasant, but the face had wisdom and authority.

A second figure entered with him, and Simon stared harder. It was a girl in her midteens, dressed as simply, but very beautiful.

6

THE PLATEAU COVERED PERHAPS FIFTY acres, and was unequally divided by an avenue leading from the main buildings. To the left there were fields, with crops under cultivation; the smaller area on the right extended to the cliff's edge and featured ornamental gardens and pools and a number of greenhouses. At the end of the avenue stood a pagoda; straightforwardly Chinese except that it was approached through a columned portico.

The man's name, they had been told, was Bei Pen, the girl's Li Mei. Simon and Brad went with them down a path through a shrubbery to an open space where there was a pool filled by a small waterfall. Troutlike fish flapped against the current, and Simon noticed a crayfish crawling among rocks at the bottom.

It was a bright morning; although the surrounding foothills were heavy with cloud, the peak of the mountain was sharp against a blue sky broken only by a few drifting puffs of white. A rustic bridge spanned the pool. It only needed a couple of doves hovering above it, Simon thought, to look like the design on a willow pattern plate. The sense of wild improbability he had felt on first seeing the bonzery came back.

Bei Pen said: "There are probably many questions you will wish to ask." Neither replied, and after a moment he went on: "Then let me question you. What do you know of the Laws of Bei-Kun?"

Simon waited for Brad to respond; this was his sort of situation. Eventually he himself said: "Not much. I know they're to do with the two minds, first mind and second mind, and the law of suggestion. And Bei Tsu mentioned other laws—far movement, far speaking. . . ."

Brad broke in: "Was that far speaking last night, when Li Mei seemed to be talking inside my head?"

Li Mei smiled slightly. She had high broad cheekbones, dark glossy hair tied back to show pretty ears, a golden skin flushing to rose. She was nothing like the women in Li Nan. And she did not teeter along in the preposterous lily walk. Her sandalled feet were small but perfectly formed.

"Yes," Bei Pen said, "that was far speaking, B'lad. As all things are, it is governed by the law of suggestion, so impeded by adverse thoughts. Your mind was more open to Li Mei than Si Mun's was to me." Simon thought: I'll bet it was! "All the laws are based on a simple truth: that there is mind in every living thing. Not just in men and women, horses, dogs, monkeys. . . . The tiniest insect has mind. Plants, too."

He touched the branch of willow which overhung the pool.

Simon asked: "Are you saying you can do this far speaking with trees?"

It came out more sceptically than he intended. Bei Pen said: "Is that so strange? Stranger than to speak with men thousands of miles away, or to see things that are happening on the far side of the world?"

There was a silence which lasted too long. Bei Pen broke it.

"We know of the place from which you come—not the land of the Lomani, but the land beyond the fireball. In his far speaking with Li Mei, B'lad revealed much."

"We were asleep," Simon said. "You can't take account of what people dream."

Ignoring that, Bei Pen said: "It explained much that might have seemed strange. Two Lomani, coming not from the west but the east, two who would not enter the deep sleep, two from whose presence the spirits of wind and fire turned away . . ."

"So you've had reports on us?" Simon said. "Was it by your order we were brought here—not the Lady Lu T'Sa's?"

"She wished your absence, we your presence: the two things went together." His eyes were searching. "Is it not true that in your own world you are familiar with the wonders I have spoken of?"

There was no point in going on denying it. Simon said, fumbling for words in Chinese to explain the difference between science and whatever kind of mysticism they went in for here: "It's different. Those wonders were—well, based on reason."

Bei Pen nodded. "And reason is a function of second mind. We talk now of first mind. Come, I will show you something."

They followed a winding path to one of the greenhouses. It was mostly stone, but the roof and south-facing wall were glazed. They went inside to warmth and a sweet pungent smell. Ripe peaches glowed against dark green leaves.

"A good crop, would you not say?" Bei Pen asked.

Simon said stubbornly: "And you say it's good because of far speaking to the plants? We get good crops in greenhouses in our land without that."

But not, he privately admitted, at anything like this altitude. He tried to reason that it was possible to breed special strains which would tolerate adverse conditions, but knew he was not convincing himself.

Without answering, Bei Pen led the way along a walk that ran through the greenhouse. As they followed him, Simon noticed something very strange: the fruits were getting less ripe and smaller. At the end there were no fruits, only trees in flower. It was impossible but also, like the elephant, undeniable.

In the middle of the day, on a terrace overlooking the fields and gardens, more than fifty men and women sat down to a simple meal of bread and crumbling white cheese and salads, washed down by a thin sharp ale. Some had come in from working in the fields. Simon realized he had been wrong in thinking the toiling figures he had seen were peasant servants. All worked for the community, and all were priests of Bei-Kun.

A large man called Bei W'ih sat opposite them. His beard was unusually full for a Chinese, black but heavily flecked with white, and he had an open jovial manner. He questioned them on the customs of the Lomani: was it true they fattened mice in pots and ate them? He also referred to stories which had reached the Middle Kingdom of a rebellion against the Lomani emperor, in which the rebels had been aided by their dead god, who gave them an all-powerful weapon and winged horses to carry them into battle. Shaking his head, he said he could believe in the mice in pots, but not so easily in the dead god and his gifts.

Simon explained that the horses did not have wings, only stirrups permitting men to fight from the saddle, and that the weapon was merely a bow, longer and deadlier than other bows.

Bei W'ih said: "And with those things, the rebels overthrew an empire which had ruled for two thousand years?" He sounded sceptical. "It is of no importance, anyway. The Western armies are a long way from the borders of the Celestial Kingdom. And arrows are feeble compared with fire darts. As for their horses, even if they were winged they would be no match for our dragons."

"Dragons?" Simon looked at him. "I mean—what are they?"

"Dragons are dragons! Have you not seen them in paintings? Winged serpents, with scaly wings and forked tails, that breathe fire."

His expression was amused, grinning almost. He clapped a hand on Simon's arm.

"Perhaps dragons do not breed in the land of the Lomani. But maybe you will have a chance to see ours. There is talk of the barbarians beyond the Wall being troublesome, and they may need chastising. Perhaps you will see our dragons fly."

. . .

A routine developed during the days that followed. Without asking, or being asked, they found themselves working in the fields and helping generally around the bonzery. It was not arduous work, and the company was pleasant. They sang a lot, and cheerfulness was the rule.

They were not invited to take part in religious ceremonies. In the early morning and again at sunset, the priests went to the pagoda and stayed for about half an hour. Individuals went there separately at other times. Simon was a bit surprised, though not unhappy about it, that they were excluded. He mentioned it to Brad: "I thought we were supposed to have been sent here for religious instruction? At least, that's what Bei Tsu told Cho-tsing."

Brad shrugged. "That was the cover story. We know now it was Bei Pen wanted us here."

"But what for? To help in the fields? It doesn't make sense."

"I suppose it will eventually."

"The guards seem to have gone back—and Bei Tsu. As far as I can see, there's nothing to stop us just walking out."

"I don't particularly want to," Brad said.

"What is it you don't want to walk out on—the bonzery, or Li Mei?"

Brad did not answer, but neither did he show any sign of rising to the remark. Simon had a feeling he had changed since they had come here. He would have expected him to be more curious about things, more inquiring. In fact, when he himself had tried to talk about the peaches Bei Pen had shown them—something which in the past would have provoked a flood of speculative argument—Brad's response had been brief and uninterested. Due to mooning after Li Mei, Simon guessed: he sat by her at meals and gravitated towards her generally. But that didn't really seem to be enough to account for the change.

Bei Pen was clearly the chief priest, or at least the acknowledged leader of the community. This was indicated by the deference and respect which were shown to him, though it was not made formal in any way. It was an attitude which Simon found himself sharing; but more than that, he became aware of a private feeling of closeness to the man. There were times when he caught himself thinking of Bei Pen almost as though he were his father.

It was a confusing and slightly bothersome feeling. He had not, in fact, ever felt particularly close to his own father, a man who treated taciturnity as one of the major virtues. It puzzled him, too, because Bei Pen had shown no special interest in him; he was amiable, but in a somewhat remote fashion, as he was to everyone.

He couldn't help wondering if it was tied up with that first encounter, with the voice in his mind as he floated in the borderland between sleep and waking. Or the illusion of the voice; he could no longer remember it vividly. He was in part glad not to recall the intrusion into his mental privacy, but the gladness was tinged with regret. Even though the impact had faded, he knew it had been an experience like nothing he had known before.

The other person in the bonzery who interested him—naturally, because she was a pretty girl—was Li Mei. On a rare occasion when Brad was not in evidence, he tried talking to her but was met with smiling indifference. One afternoon, rather to his surprise, he found himself discussing the subject with Bei Pen.

He had met him returning from the pagoda.

Bei Pen asked where B'lad was, and Simon said he had gone off with Li Mei.

"It seems she prefers your friend. Does that trouble you?"

"I'm not sure." He paused. "No, I don't think it does."

That surprised him, too, when he thought about it. There had been rivalries between himself and Brad over girls in the past, and he really ought to feel more strongly about this one's indifference. But he didn't; in a way, there was a sense of relief. He shook his head.

"I don't know why."

"The affinities between male and female come from first mind. They have nothing to do with reason, much with illusion."

"First mind, second mind . . . I still don't understand."

Patiently Bei Pen explained. First mind was the mind of God, the creator of the universe; and also the root of all living things which God had created. Second mind, the seat of awareness, of reasoning, was in the brain, and died when the brain died. First mind, like God, was immortal.

"It sounds the same as in our religion, except that instead of first mind and second mind we talk about body and soul. Well, soul and body."

"I know of your Christian beliefs," Bei Pen said. "There are similarities. But Christians hold that only men and women have souls. That is arrogant; and untrue."

Disinclined for religious argument, Simon found distraction in the clouds billowing in over the plateau. It was the first time the blue sky had been invaded since their arrival.

He said: "It looks as though it might rain."

Bei Pen nodded. "The crops require it."

Brad came indoors when the rain started, looking cheerful.

Simon asked: "Where's Li Mei?"

"She went to the pagoda."

"What *does* go on there? Do you know?"

"No."

It was a negative which declared not so much ignorance as total lack of interest. Simon said: "I wonder what's inside—some sort of temple?"

Brad shrugged, indifferently.

Simon felt exasperation building up. He said: "What's *wrong* with you, Brad?"

"With me? Nothing's wrong."

"You were always the one who asked the questions. I can't think why you've stopped."

"You can ask too many questions," Brad said. "Maybe I'm learning."

It rained steadily for the rest of the day and throughout the night; but next morning the sky was once again clear and blue. Brad disappeared after breakfast, presumably in search of Li Mei. Simon could have joined one of the work parties, but didn't. This was not from idleness. He had a feeling of restlessness and unease. Though there was nothing to be uneasy about: the sun was warm, the mountain air invigorating—all round there was brightness and peace.

He was standing by one of the pools, watching fish move lazily in the clear water, when he sensed a nearby presence. Looking back, he saw Bei Pen.

He was aware of mixed feelings—a reinforcement simultaneously of the uneasiness and the sense of well-being. Chiefly the latter. But at the same time there was an urge towards contrariness, defiance.

When Bei Pen greeted him, he said, roughly, almost rudely: "Those magic tricks Bei Tsu was trying to do at the palace—can you do them?"

He thought Bei Pen might object to his tone, or the use of the word *tricks*. But he merely smiled. "When it is necessary. And appropriate."

"Do some now." He felt keyed up. "Please."

The last word came out more as challenge than request. Bei Pen did not reply. Simon felt resentful, but at the same time a little ashamed. He started to turn away, but out of the corner of his eye saw something move on the surface of the pool: an eddying mist which curdled into smoke and slowly rose. Shapes formed—indeterminate at first, but resolving into things with wings and small round bodies and little quivering heads. They were dull green in colour.

It was a moment of wonder, but he refused to accept it. He stared at the shapes, concentrating the refusal, focusing scepticism like a laser beam. And it worked. He saw them shimmer, start dissolving at their edges. One or two disappeared; the rest were mottled with transparency.

Then, as on the first night in the bonzery, the voice was inside his head, benevolent and sure: "Peace, and the mingling of minds . . ."

It was possible to resist it. He knew that, but even as he framed that possibility, something within him rejected it. He heard his own mind whispering back: "Peace . . . and the mingling of minds."

The winged creatures were whole again; and not dull green but a dozen different colours, throwing off iridescences in their kaleidoscopic flight.

He looked from them to Bei Pen, involuntarily smiling. Bei Pen smiled back. The creatures buzzed about his head, their wings beating to a cadence which sang in his ears. They had a smell of wild-flowers, and he felt them brush against his cheek and forehead. So they *were* real—perceptible through sight, hearing, smell, touch, every sense except taste. And, as he thought that, one hovered before his mouth, probing, and there was honey on his lips.

7

NEXT DAY, SIMON TALKED BRAD INTO taking a walk outside the bonzery. Li Mei was missing and had been all morning, but Brad was still less than keen. In Brad's present mood, Simon felt pressure of any kind might be counterproductive. He limited himself simply to asking Brad to come with him, as a favour almost. Brad agreed without enthusiasm.

They went down the hill to where the white goats grazed, and on the way Simon told him about the episode beside the pool. He said: "I had this feeling— that I could stop it all happening if I wanted to. And

I did want to, in a way. But there was this other feeling of being part of it, of helping to make the flying things. It felt good."

Brad was silent.

Simon said: "What bothers me is whether Bei Pen has some sort of power over me, and if so, how much."

"Does it matter? He hasn't tried to get you to do anything you don't want to, has he?"

"It matters," Simon said. "Something happened that first night. I don't know what, but I know it matters. You must see that."

He was trying to provoke Brad into an argument. It was extraordinary that any trying should be required: Brad was normally ready and willing to argue about anything under the sun. But not now. He said nothing; merely stared down the slope towards the mist which clung to the hillside as it had done the afternoon they had come through it and seen the bonzery.

Simon said sharply: "It was some sort of telepathic contact, and it didn't stop at that. In my case with Bei Pen, and in yours with Li Mei."

Brad turned towards him.

"What sort of power does she have over you?"

"Don't be stupid!"

"I'm not being stupid. I admit I don't know what's happening. Why won't you?"

"Because it's entirely different."

"Tell me how."

"It's obvious how. Bei Pen's the head priest here. It's reasonable you might feel worried about being influenced in some way. Li Mei's not much older than we are—if she is older."

"But all the same . . ."

"All the same nothing!"

Brad's tetchiness was close to explosion, and provoking that wouldn't be any help.

Simon let a pause go by, and said: "I wonder how Cho-tsing's getting on?"

"All right, I should think."

"I was wondering about possibly going back to Li Nan. I still don't know why we were brought here, but we aren't doing anything, are we? There's no reason why we shouldn't go back."

"The Lady Lu T'Sa might not be keen on it."

"But the Lord Chancellor might. She said we had to go to the Bonzery of Grace—well, we've done

that. I'd like to see Cho-tsing's monkeys again. And
Cho-tsing."

Brad said abruptly: "I'm going back to the
bonzery."

He turned and went, plainly neither expecting
nor wanting Simon to follow. A few yards away, a
goat stood, bland and yellow-eyed, chewing and
staring.

Simon said: "You don't give a lot, either, do
you?"

After supper, Simon played chess with Bei W'ih. He
started well, but after about twenty moves the big
bearded man lured him into a trap which cost him
his queen, and the result subsequently was never in
doubt. Checkmating him, Bei W'ih said: "Another
game, Si Mun?"

"Not right now. I'm not up to your standard.
You ought to take on B'lad."

"He is skilled at chess?"

"Much more than I am."

"But he is not here."

"No."

"He plays, perhaps, with Li Mei."

His tone was part questioning, part amused. Simon did not reply; he liked Bei W'ih, but did not want to discuss Brad with him.

Gathering up the chess pieces, Bei W'ih said: "I told you there might be a chance to see our dragons fly. Word has come from the commander of the army of the north. There will be action soon, against the barbarians. In a few days, I shall be leaving the bonzery to go to him. If you wish, you may come with me. Your friend, B'lad, also."

He dropped the pieces in their box and shut the lid.

"Think about it, Si Mun. This may be good, for both of you."

He thought about it a lot, and the next morning spoke to Bei Pen. He felt a prickle of apprehension as he broached the subject and found himself stumbling over his words. Would Bei Pen be willing to let them go? And if he weren't, just how would the prohibition be expressed? As he had said to Brad, there seemed to be no constraints on them—they could wander about the bonzery or out of it as they pleased—but it suddenly occurred to him that constraints did not have to be visible or take the form of guards. He had a

fearful thought of the voice in his head, not just for-
bidding but paralysing his will—even changing it,
making him not want to go.

But Bei Pen, after listening without comment,
said: "You ask this on behalf of B'lad, also?"

"Yes."

"Have you spoken of it with him?"

"Not yet."

"Then do so. It was courteous of you to ask, but
unnecessary. You are free to do as you wish."

"I was wondering. . . ." Simon hesitated.

"What?"

"If perhaps it could be—well, could come as an
order from you."

"You know it could not. That would be deceit.
And would serve no purpose. Speak to your friend.
You are both free."

That day was a holiday, with the minimum of work
done and various forms of recreation. Some of the
men engaged in wrestling bouts and contests with
wooden staves; and both men and women took part
in dances and flew kites, which soared like angular
birds above the chasm bordering the plateau.

Watching them with Brad, Simon said: "There's a powerful updraft, of course."

"Yes."

"Did you do any kite flying when you were a kid?"

"Some."

"Mine either refused to take off or went straight into a tree. The original Charlie Brown."

Brad smiled but did not answer.

There was no point, Simon decided, in hanging back. He said: "I spoke to Bei Pen earlier on." It came out more forcefully than he intended.

Brad looked at him, but incuriously.

Simon went on to tell of Bei W'ih's offer. "I still don't know what these dragons are he's talking about, but the whole thing should be interesting. I'd like to see how the Chinese army rates. Anyway, Bei Pen has no objection."

He realized Brad was not paying even a minimum of attention and at the same time became aware of Li Mei approaching. She smiled, at Brad exclusively, and put out her small white hands to grasp his. Yes, she was beautiful, he thought; but beautiful like a picture or a piece of sculpture.

Holding hands with Brad, she led the way along

a path that turned and dipped behind a rocky bluff. Despite a strong sense of being unwanted, Simon followed them. There was a pool with the inevitable willow and a large smooth boulder by the edge which provided a seat for two. Simon had to stand. He decided attack was the best policy and said: "Brad and I were talking about leaving the bonzery."

To his surprise, Li Mei smiled, this time at him. In her little lilting voice, she said: "I think you are right. We should leave the bonzery."

He was disconcerted. "But . . . *you* can't."

The smile remained, but lost any hint of humour. She said in a quiet cold voice: "I do as I wish, Si Mun."

He turned from her to Brad. "It's crazy. We're talking about joining up with the army. There'll probably be fighting—certainly we'll be living rough. No way a life for a girl. Tell her she has to stay here."

Brad did not reply.

Li Mei said: "No one tells me what to do or not to do. No one."

A voice came from behind them: Bei Pen's. "Even though others may not command one, right thinking must."

. . .

He came towards them. "These young people have been our guests," he said, "but they do not belong here. It is proper that they should go their ways now."

"They are free to choose," Li Mei said. She looked at Simon. "Is it your wish to leave the bonzery?"

Simon nodded. "I think it's time we left."

"And you, B'lad?"

"Yes." He paused. "If you come with us."

Li Mei turned to Bei Pen. "They have made their choices, each of them."

Bei Pen shook his head. "This is wrong, and you know it."

"I don't see what's wrong," Brad said. "We don't have to go with Bei W'ih. We can go anywhere, and I don't see why Li Mei shouldn't come with us."

Bei Pen kept his eyes on Li Mei. "As you know, I have no power to command you. But I ask you to remember what is proper. You know the laws. You know that wrong thinking must be rejected."

"Your wrong may be my right. I am free to choose."

"You may be." He pointed to Brad. "But what of him?"

"You have heard him speak."

"In illusion there is no freedom. Release him."

It was just a girl, defying the so-called wisdom of the older generation, Simon thought—nothing unusual in that. But even so, and on this day of sun-lit calm with not even a breeze to ruffle the willow leaves, he had a feeling of darkness and coldness and storm.

Li Mei said: "Illusion is a mighty emperor. As *you* know. Let us be, Bei Pen."

"I cannot command you." He looked old and tired against the freshness of her youth. "But I can set him free, if you will not."

Her smile was scornful. "You can do nothing."

Bei Pen took a step towards her, and their gazes locked. There was nothing remarkable about that, either, Simon told himself: just two people staring into one another's eyes. But as moments passed, he started to feel uncomfortable. Something was happening behind the clash of gazes—something silent and invisible, but deep and momentous. There was strain in both their faces, and in Li Mei's a savagery which astonished and unnerved him. The feeling of discomfort became stronger; oppressive, almost painful. He wanted to say something to break the dreadful stillness, yet could not.

But Brad did. In a strangled voice, he cried: "Stop it! Let her alone."

Simon saw Bei Pen's gaze waver. In Li Mei's face, the savagery turned into a hideous look of triumph. It frightened him. She was winning, and he knew her victory meant appalling disaster, not just for Brad but for all of them.

Then Bei Pen's gaze fixed again and held, in a concentration that seemed to turn his face to stone. And Li Mei's grimace of triumph started to change, too. It grew uglier and harsher, and there was pain in it and a dawning recognition of defeat. Not just her expression but her actual face was altering, as though Bei Pen's eyes were a brush, with power to erase her features and redraw them. She turned from girl into woman, and the woman was not young but old, and then older.

Brad cried out again, but Bei Pen showed no sign of hearing him. His whole body was rigid as a statue.

It was as though Li Mei was emerging from a chrysalis, but what emerged was nothing like a butterfly. Her skin turned to wrinkled parchment as her body shrank and humped into that of an incredibly ancient woman. How ancient, Simon wondered in horror? Older, certainly, than any human being he had seen or could imagine seeing.

And she knew what was happening to her. She gave a cry, a croak rather, of rage and anguish from a palsied throat, and took a step forward, clawlike hands outstretched. It was that tottering step which drew Simon's eyes down to her feet—tiny and misshapen: bound.

He thought she was going to throw herself at Bei Pen; but instead she veered away and ran, in the graceless teetering lily walk, along the path and out of sight.

There was no colour in Brad's face.

Simon asked: "Who is she?"

Bei Pen looked drawn and spent. He spoke slowly, as though telling a tale that had once been familiar, but very long ago.

"Legend has it that Bei-Kun came to the Celestial Kingdom from a distant land. After long years of meditation, he proclaimed the Laws. He had many disciples, but two of these—a brother and sister—

were especially close. When in the fulness of time he bade farewell to his other disciples, and went up into the mountains, he took those two with him.

"When they did not return, it was thought they had died in the mountains. But they did not die. In very ancient days, long before Bei-Kun, the followers of Tao held that thought and meditation could yield extraordinary powers, including the power of keeping death at bay. But although such things were taught, no one before Bei-Kun achieved them. And he kept the knowledge to himself and his two disciples."

"Why?" Simon asked.

"Because such powers can have evil consequences as well as good."

"But Bei-Kun and his two disciples had them?"

"They learned other things, too. They discovered how to create illusions in the minds of others by far thinking. Even though they kept death at bay, their bodies aged; but they could put on the appearance of youth. When at last they came down from the mountains, they were not recognized and could take up a new life in a new generation.

"There were many times of going away and

coming back. But a long life does not always bring wisdom, or contentment. It can lead to emptiness of spirit and despair. At the last going away, one of the disciples preferred death. That, too, is not difficult to accomplish."

"And the other disciple," Simon said, "was Li Mei?"

"Yes. They were close in spirit, and one despair leads to another. And despair can take strange forms."

"But your power is greater than hers, isn't it?"

He nodded. "Yes."

"Because you are the one who discovered the Laws and proclaimed them. You are Bei-Kun."

Bei Pen did not answer. He turned and walked away. His appearance was still that of a man in late middle age, but it could not disguise an aching weariness. Simon felt pity and affection, an urge to go after him. But Brad was his first concern.

"That was a terrible thing to have to see," he said. "But how could anyone live like it—putting a mask on over a face scarcely better than a skull?"

"Suggestion rules." Brad's voice was tight and dry. "Isn't that one of the laws of Bei-Kun? And there's no real difference between suggestion and illusion, when you come down to it."

"But when you've seen the reality . . ."

"What is reality? What we saw just now or the way I remember her? If I close my eyes, I can see her again. As she was. Which is the real Li Mei?"

"You *saw* what the reality was. That hideous old woman. And then when she ran off, on those terrible little twisted feet . . ."

"Forget it!"

"But once you know it, you can't forget it. That's the whole point."

Brad walked away. Simon did not try to follow him. The shock had been shattering, but shocks wore off. He would see things more clearly in the morning.

Brad was silent that evening and ate nothing at supper. Neither Bei Pen nor Li Mei put in an appearance. The rest seemed unaware of anything wrong; Bei W'ih jested about Brad's lack of appetite.

During the night, Simon was aware of Brad tossing and turning. He thought he would be unable to get to sleep himself; then dropped into an oblivion interrupted by nightmares in which people wearing masks stripped them off to show hideous faces; and the faces, too, were masks, to be stripped again, revealing greater horror still . . . and so on and on, endlessly.

The sky was quite light when he awoke and looked across to Brad. The other mat was empty.

8

SIMON ASKED BEI PEN: "WILL YOU SEND someone after them?"

"It would serve no purpose."

"You could have him brought back."

"Supposing they could be found, in the first place. The bounds of the Middle Kingdom are wide. And would he thank me for it? Or thank you?"

"He doesn't know what he's doing. He needs protection from the illusion she puts into his mind. Protection against himself, if you like."

"In sleep, first mind is defenceless against the

dreams that invade it. But B'lad was not sleeping when he went away with Li Mei."

"But he doesn't have the powers she has!"

"True. And that is why I broke the illusion for him. It was not easy, and the consequences are immeasurable."

"You may have broken it, but obviously it's come back."

"There is a difference. Now he knows it to be an illusion, even though he embraces it."

"But can't you do something about that?" Simon tried, hopelessly, to think of a Chinese word for *deprogramming*. "Through the law of suggestion?"

"A puppet pulled by different strings is still a puppet. It may be that in the end he will reject illusion. But only he can do it."

"If you won't do anything," Simon said, "I shall. At least I can go and look for him." He stared at Bei Pen. "You won't try to stop me?"

Bei Pen inclined his head. "No one will."

Bei W'ih said: "I leave in the morning. Are you coming with me, Si Mun?"

"No."

The big man looked speculatively at him. "I looked to have two companions. First, one is lost and now, it seems, the other. Your friend follows a will-o'-the-wisp. What is it you have decided you would rather do than watch my dragons fly?"

"I'm going after him."

"And which road will you travel?"

Simon did not answer.

"If you go south and they have gone north, it will be a long journey. And every crossroads can lead you further astray."

He came to Simon and put an arm around his shoulders.

"It is understandable that you should wish to find your friend, and proper. But let us apply second mind to the situation and think rationally. You could wander for years and find yourself further off at the end. It is better to be in one place and listen to what travels on the wind. The army has scouts and spies by the thousand. If their eyes and ears do not bring news of him, nothing can. And meanwhile"—he grinned—"you will see the dragons."

• • •

They travelled very light, taking no rations. Everywhere, at the sight of the blue priestly robes, the villagers brought out the best of their food and drink. On the third night, at a large village in the rich farming land of the plain, a banquet was provided by the local mandarin.

As the long succession of exotic dishes wound towards an end, Simon became aware of an atmosphere of expectancy. When the lamps were being extinguished, he guessed what it was about: a magic show like the one Bei Tsu had failed to perform at the palace. His guess was confirmed when the last lamps were put out and Bei W'ih brought out two rods from his pouch and started to twirl them.

They seemed to be tipped with a phosphorescent material: the twirlings made arcs and twists and circles of luminescence in the darkness. And Bei W'ih began to tell a tale, a flight of fancy involving a noble hero, pure and lovely maiden, wicked villain, and a host of minor characters.

The twirlings continued all the while—pretty, Simon thought, but pointless. But the audience, as he realized from their vigorous expressions of approval, horror, anger, were getting a lot more out of the proceedings than he was. The tale wound to its climax, signalled by a delirious twinkling dance of lights, which was greeted with sustained and rapturous applause.

As their mules jogged along next day, Simon asked: "The storytelling is something expected?"

"Hoped for, shall we say? And so provided, in return for hospitality."

"And shaking the rods is a necessary part?"

Bei W'ih looked at him. "When the rods danced, what did you see?"

"Moving lights."

"The others saw much more: men fighting, a boy and girl embracing, a boat buffeted by rough waters on a river flowing between high cliffs, dragons soaring through skies pierced by lightning bolts. . . ."

"So the lights were helping you to create illusions which they believed?"

"Yes. But illusions which existed for me, too. I saw all those things. But not for you, Si Mun? I wonder why. Because you are of the Lomani? But you are not the first such to visit the Celestial Kingdom and witness its wonders. Others have seen the pictures. I wonder why not you?"

Simon did not reply. It was interesting, he reflected, that this time the illusions had worked for others, if not for him. Maybe his negative vibes were getting less powerful—as a result of his contacts with Bei Pen? It was just as well anyway: the villagers might have been less civilized than the members of the imperial court about losing their evening's entertainment. They jogged on in silence.

Twelve days later, at a point where the rough track they were following crested a hilltop, they came in sight of the Wall. Simon had been prepared to be impressed, but the actuality bludgeoned him. No pictures in books or on television had adequately prepared him for the impact of the vast bulwark of stone striding across the valley floor and climbing hundreds of feet over the next hill.

He remembered reading somewhere that even in his own world this had been the only work of man visible from the Moon. And here it was no crumbling ruin but an artifact in good repair and in use— he could see the heads of a troop of soldiers bobbing above the battlement as they marched towards the fort at the top of the hill. There banners, twisting in a stiff breeze, decorated a central tower. A stream ran through a culvert beneath it, and huts stretched away on either side to form a straggling village.

They were respectfully greeted and taken to a room looking south along the valley towards hazily sunlit hills. They were brought water and oils for washing, and a change of linen. Tea with the General followed.

He was short even for a Chinese, but colourful in a scarlet robe trimmed with jade and silver, and his wispy beard had been lacquered into the shape of an out-thrust dagger. He had deep-set eyes which darted, quickly and penetratingly, to whatever took his attention. Although small in stature, he was well muscled; as a bare arm demonstrated. His appearance, Simon thought, could be called birdlike, but the bird was a fighting cock.

Following the formalities of the tea ceremony, practical considerations formed the basis for discussion. Over recent years, the barbarians had grown increasingly troublesome. In the previous six months, they had destroyed several villages north of the Wall and, in one impudent invasion of the sacred territory of the Celestial Kingdom, three south of it.

It would not, the General said, have been difficult to move at once against those daring to encroach on the domain of the Son of Heaven, and destroy them; but he felt a more signal retribution was appropriate. Spies reported that the barbarians, flushed with their success, were moving south in great numbers and that a large-scale invasion was intended.

Bei W'ih asked: "Is it good terrain for dragons?"

"There are three valleys through which the lawless ones might come south. One of these, the Valley of Winds, is excellent dragon country. The remaining two will be strongly defended. They will come, therefore, through the Valley of Winds."

Bei W'ih nodded. "How soon?"

"We can choose the moment to lance the boil. A weak assault will lure them into counterattack. Defences at the valley's entrance will also be weak. Three miles in, the valley narrows, and if battle is joined there, retreat will not be easy. There will be estimable slaughter."

During the days that followed, Simon had time on his hands. As long as he wore the robe marking him as an acolyte to the priesthood, he was treated with wary respect; but when he changed it for an ordinary tunic, the men of the garrison proved more amiable. It was not very different from being in a Roman military station. There were the same grouses, the same distractions—above all, the same resignation, stemming from the realization that others were in charge of one's destiny, and that there was nothing to do about that but grin and bear it.

He felt he might have adjusted to the situation and settled down, except for worrying about Brad and wondering what might have happened to him. He still found it difficult to accept what had happened—that Brad, whom he had thought of as both brighter and more level-headed than himself, should have done something so totally irrational. There was obviously a compulsive element in his behaviour, like a moth pursuing a flame. But a moth had no brain, and this particular flame, as had been so clearly and shockingly demonstrated, was nothing but an ugly guttering candle.

He could not believe that Brad would not, sooner or later, free himself from the net of fantasy Li Mei had thrown over him. But he felt also that there should be some way in which he could help. He hadn't made much impression on Brad at the bonzery, but if he were in a position to keep on hammering away it must be possible to do something. The difficulty about that was that he needed to be with Brad to exercise persuasion, and he didn't have the remotest idea where Brad might be. He reminded Bei W'ih of his promise of using the army's sources of information to help trace Brad. Bei W'ih told him instructions had gone out; but reminded him in turn that the Middle Kingdom was a vast country.

He also found himself missing Bei Pen. In the first days after leaving the bonzery, he had had a sense of relief: each mile they travelled made him more confident that his mind was his own again, free of external intervention either for good or ill. But here, without the distractions of travelling, his thoughts often went to Bei Pen and, at times, with a recollection that pierced and troubled him, to the strange mental closeness they had shared. He both wished for and dreaded its renewal.

Altogether he was glad when rumours of impending action began to circulate and still gladder when the army finally moved.

He resumed his acolyte's robe and travelled with Bei W'ih in the rear of the long column of men and horses and wagons. They took a separate course on reaching the Valley of Winds; their mules laboured up a steep and stony track, which led them to a village several hundred feet above the valley's floor. Almost directly below lay the narrower section of which the General had spoken.

In the morning, Bei W'ih chose a position on a spur some distance from the village. The night had been dry, and the tops of the hills were etched by the glow from the still unrisen sun. A coruscation of campfires glimmered beneath them. Bei W'ih pointed north. Far off, at the mouth of the valley, there was movement: it looked like a horde of trekking insects, dimly visible in the half-light.

Simon had seen armies moving into battle before, but always as a prelude to action in which he himself would be involved. His chief concern had been with the part he was going to play, with excitement and apprehension warring in his mind. In this case, he was condemned to be a spectator. Although they looked like insects from this vantage point, he knew they were men—men who would soon be joined in a frenzy of bloodletting with those other men now munching breakfast beside the campfires. He had an unhappy consciousness of the absurdity of it all. He said to Bei W'ih: "You came to help win a battle. Is there no way of preventing the battle taking place?"

Bei W'ih looked at him. "Would you have me make an end of the follies of mankind? Have they learned that secret in the land you come from, Si Mun?"

"These dragons of yours—if they showed their power *before* the fighting started . . ."

Bei W'ih shook his head. "There are no easy ways. And all has to be repeated, over and over, until men find wisdom, or time itself ends."

The advancing line halted about a hundred yards from the opposing ranks, and a bombardment started. Both sides had field artillery: cannons boomed, sending dark specks of cannonballs hurtling through the air, and there were the fiery streaks of rocket arrows. The remote thin cries of the wounded punctuated the deeper din. After about half an hour, the interchange died away; there was silence apart from distant moans of pain, and everything seemed frozen into tranquillity. Then, from a rattle of orders, movement began again. The gap between the lines narrowed and disappeared. There was the sudden roar of men hiding their fears in anger.

The imperial troops wore green uniforms. Simon saw patches of green encircled and swallowed up, the green line generally falling back. Unexpectedly he had a feeling of partisanship, an urge to be down there fighting with them. He said urgently: "What about the dragons?"

"Look."

His eye followed Bei W'ih's pointing finger. In the rear of the imperial army, objects were rising into the sky. They were in a multiplicity of colours—scarlet and yellow, blue and green and vermilion. They had tails trailing behind them and crudely shaped heads. Even so far away, he could see just how crude, and could recognize the constructions of paper and bamboo, flying from strings. They were kites.

It was ludicrous—a line of kites flying above forces locked in desperate battle. He said disbelievingly: "Is *that* what you call dragons?"

"Watch."

Carried on a stiff breeze, they advanced steadily

as the lines controlling them were paid out. They soared above the rear guard of the imperial army and onwards over the fighting. At the same time, the noise of battle had a new cacophony added to it: of gongs, trumpets, rattles, exploding crackers. There was a surge of whiteness like a wave, as thousands of faces turned upwards to the sky. Then a yell of despair, an answering shout of triumph, and the barbarians broke and ran, with the victorious greens pursuing them.

Bei W'ih turned to Simon. "Well?"

"I saw what happened. I don't know why it did."

"For you there were no dragons, only kites. But there was nothing for you when my bright sticks danced for the villagers. There are things you do not see."

"That was in a darkened room, with only twenty or thirty people."

Bei W'ih smiled. "You seek to put limits to something you do not understand. There is also expectation."

"Expectation?"

"The dragons have flown before. Not in every battle, but the tales are told, from generation to generation, of how, when the Son of Heaven's need is great, his dragons fly over his warriors and scatter his foes. So in the minds of all, there is that hope, that dread."

Simon began to see, vaguely, how it might work. The stress of battle could have strange effects on the human mind, as he knew from experience. The imperial army must have spies in the barbarian ranks. If they were ready to raise the panic cry of "Dragons!" at a critical moment—at the same time as the gongs and trumpets and crackers went off—it could induce mass hysteria, maybe a mass hallucination. He asked: "What if the imperial army were faced by an enemy that didn't know the legend of the dragons?"

"There is no such enemy."

"Not now, perhaps. But maybe in the future."

Bei W'ih smiled his disbelief.

"The army that conquered Rome might march east."

"Their feet would be sore after such a march, if they were not worn away. And it would make no difference."

"Why not?"

"Because the dragons would still be real for our

soldiers. Who can suffer defeat when the Emperor's dragons ride the skies above him?"

Simon saw the point: the roar of triumph had been louder than the cry of despair. Bei W'ih was right. It wasn't easy to set limits to the power of illusion.

9

THE VICTORY BANQUET BEGAN WITH THE sun still high above the valley's western escarpment and went on until the night was heavy with stars. Simon and Bei W'ih sat with the General and his senior officers beneath an awning lined with green velvet, open to the air and to the songs and laughter of the increasingly drunken soldiery. Many of the officers were drunk, too, though Simon noticed that the General limited his consumption of the freely flowing rice wine to small sips in response to toasts. There were plenty of those, and all were coupled with the long life and health of the glorious Son of Heaven.

Sipping himself, Simon thought of the thin boy, weighed down by gold-embroidered robes. Remembering the Roman custom of triumphs, he wondered if there might be a possibility of the General taking his victorious army back to parade it through the imperial city. It would give him a chance of seeing Cho-tsing again. It might also provide the opportunity for getting a better line on Brad's possible whereabouts. Cho-tsing, he was sure, would be willing to help, and the government's spy network must be far more extensive than the army's.

This possibility, though, was knocked on the head when the General began talking to Bei W'ih of his plans for the future. He intended to move his army north of the Wall for a spell. It was known which villages had given aid and comfort to the barbarians. And it was proper that the Emperor's displeasure should be made plain and that they should be reminded of his might.

Bei W'ih agreed that such action was justified and might well be of value in persuading the villagers to resist evil suggestions in the future.

The General said: "And what of you, priest of

Bei-Kun—will you return now to the Bonzery of Grace?"

"Yes. My dragons are no longer needed and will not be for many years, I hope."

"And will you take this young Lomani with you?"

His tone was speculative. Both men looked at Simon.

In a neutral voice, Bei W'ih said: "He has taken no vows."

"If you have no objection," the General said, "and it is the young Lomani's wish, I could find him employment here with the army."

"Would it be your wish, Si Mun, to accept a post in the service of the Lord General?" Bei W'ih asked.

They both looked at Simon with courteous attention. It sounded like the offer of a choice, but Simon knew better than to think the choice was free. What surprised him was that the General, who had shown no particular sign of interest, should want to keep him; but if he did, it was elementary common sense to go along with that.

And in fact from his own point of view, it wasn't a bad idea. Not as good as going to Li Nan would have been, but better on the whole than going back to the bonzery, knowing Brad would not be there. There was also the unresolved problem of his relationship with Bei Pen. The authority he would be under here, however irksome, would not touch his mind.

He bowed to the general. "I shall be most humbly grateful for the opportunity to perform any service Your Highness may require of me."

Bei W'ih, when they said good-bye next morning, said: "It is likely to be a long time before we meet again, if we ever do. I shall miss you, Si Mun, but this is a better thing for you. I do not think you would have been suited to life as a priest."

"If any word of B'lad reaches the bonzery . . ."

"It will be sent on to you without delay." He pressed Simon's shoulder. "The Great Spirit be with you."

In the succeeding days, Simon acquired a better understanding of the General. Initially he had formed the view that he was intelligent, but also a vain man and a martinet. Closer acquaintance confirmed the opinion, but with interesting modifications. The intelligence, for instance, was wider ranging and less fettered than he would have expected in a military mind; and the vanity was actually founded on a diffidence about his personal appearance, which was almost endearing.

For instance, he was very much aware of his lack of height and, on ceremonial occasions, wore boots with raised soles which gave him a curious clumping walk. But this led him to admire taller men rather than resenting them. In fact it was probably Simon's own tallness—he stood seven or eight inches higher than the General—which had attracted his interest. He had an extensive collection of different uniforms and an even wider selection of hats, some of which were very ornate. Before leaving his quarters, he invariably made a close examination of his image in a glass; yet the peering inspection was not self-congratulatory but anxious.

As to the martinet aspect, he was certainly a disciplinarian but, Simon realized, a reluctant one. When a soldier had to be flogged—for drunkenness which had led to the wounding of one of his companions—Simon was aware that the gaudy little man by his side, though outwardly grim-looking, was liking it as little as he did and was heartily glad when the ceremony was over. And the punitive parties which were sent against the villages north of the Wall were given specific instructions to spare women and children.

The brightness of mind, and voracious appetite for information which went with it, had probably also formed part of his motivation in commandeering Simon's services. Now that campaigning was over and he had more time on his hands, he was able to pursue an interest in Simon's Lomani background. The questions he put were pertinent and searching, especially on military subjects.

They had some long discussions on the differences between Eastern and Western methods of waging war; and his attitude, unlike Bei W'ih's, was not contemptuous but curious. If there was anything at all to be gleaned which might improve the effectiveness of the forces of the Celestial One, he was determined to ferret it out.

Simon said: "But you don't need new weapons, do you, when you have the dragons?"

He no longer called him Highness when they were alone. The General shook his head, brandishing his beard.

"No superiority over the enemy is ever enough. For want of a dagger, an empire may be lost."

"We have a similar saying, about a horseshoe nail. But even without the dragons, your weapons are so much better than those in the West. They have nothing like your cannons and fire darts." A thought struck him. "You also have steam wagons, which they do not. Have you never thought of using them in battle?"

The general shook his head dismissively. "They might be of use if battles took place in cities or along roads. But they are fought on rough ground, where wagons cannot go."

"They could be made to."

"How?"

Simon began outlining the principle of caterpillar traction. He didn't find it easy, especially in Chinese, but the General was quick on the uptake. He said, when he had finally grasped the idea: "Have you seen such wagons, in the West?"

Simon shook his head, crossing his fingers.

"So, you are an inventor! I was right to keep you with me, young Lomani. It may be you will do good service to the Emperor."

His tone was warmly admiring. Simon had a moment of embarrassment about accepting praise, but decided he had little choice. In fact, he might as well go the whole hog and invent the tank completely.

"You could also put plates of steel around the wagon, and on top of it . . ."

Following this conversation, Simon's status rose considerably. He was provided with a team of Chinese craftsmen, who were both attentive and diligent. Too attentive in some ways. They put intelligent and awkward questions, and he was soon made aware of the difference between a general idea, in his case vaguely remembered, and its specific applications.

He knew that the basis of caterpillar traction was that you had two continuous tracks, made up of individual plates joined together to form a pair of endless chains encircling wheels on either side of the vehicle. Given the relatively advanced stage of Chinese metallurgy, and the high level of local craftsmanship, this did not prove difficult to achieve. The prototype tank which was produced, however, was a total flop: it clanked and hissed but did not move an inch.

Fortunately the Chinese engineers were brighter than he was in analysing the problem. They were using the same kind of steam engine as powered the steam wagons. They worked it out that the inertia to be overcome to move a tracked vehicle was inevitably greater than in the case of a vehicle moving on wheels and on a reasonably level surface. A higher pressure of steam, they calculated, was the answer. Several exploded boilers later, they achieved that, and the tank rolled.

It did not roll far, coming to a halt on the first attempt to climb rising ground. Here again Simon's bafflement was compensated for by the resourcefulness of his artificers. They worked out the answer, which was to have the tracks so mounted that the front ends rose and fell independently of one another. The tank climbed a hill to the accompaniment of cheers and clapping. The applause was directed towards Simon, and he acknowledged it modestly. Honour, in the Chinese system, clearly went to the boss man, whoever put the real work in. On reflection, he decided that was not so very different from the system in the world he had grown up in. Wherever you were, if you got lucky, you got lucky. No point in arguing about that.

Summer passed into autumn, the days shortening and occasional mornings sharp with frost. At intervals of approximately two weeks, a troop of horsemen brought a courier from the imperial court: he stayed overnight and the following day returned to Li Nan with the General's current report. Although the General was well supplied with scribes, he wrote the reports himself, filling a scroll with elegant characters. He was extremely proud of his calligraphy.

The General told Simon, when the tank was finally working properly, that he had reported this remarkable achievement to the Celestial One. He also hinted at the possibility of an imperial reward to the inventor, and that the Emperor's bounty could be generous. Having decided to accept anything that came his way, Simon awaited the next arrival of the courier with interest. It also occurred to him that if the reports actually got to the Emperor, instead of being picked up by the Lord Chancellor or the Dowager Empress, he might get some personal message from Cho-tsing. He was bound to identify this Si Mun with the one who had for a time been his companion.

The moon had been new for the last visit from the courier, so his return was expected at the full. When that passed and the moon was five days into the wane, it was obvious something was wrong. The most likely explanation, in the General's view, was that the troop had been attacked by bandits. It was extremely rare for bandits to have the temerity to assail those who carried the Emperor's banner, but unfortunately not completely unknown. He recalled an instance from his own early days as a soldier; he had been part of the force which traced the miscreants to their mountain lair and slaughtered them to a man.

Simon asked: "Will you be sending a party out from here?"

The General looked slightly shocked. "To anticipate the wishes of the Son of Heaven would be almost as improper as disobeying them. A report will have gone back to Li Nan from one of the staging posts. Orders will be sent."

He would never, Simon thought, be able to fathom the intricacies of Chinese etiquette, either military or civil. Changing the subject, he reported that the tank was ready for further trials. They went on horseback to the spot, farther up the valley, where the workshop had been set up. It was a winter morning, with snow blurring the outlines of the surrounding hills and a few specks drifting down from a sullen sky.

The new trials were on the tank's offensive possibilities. It was manned by soldiers who tried out a variety of weapons—muskets and fire arrows and even a small cannon—as the tank rolled along. They were aiming at targets set on the hillside, and the result was a fiasco: not one was hit, and the results were completely erratic. What was needed, Simon realized, was to have the weapons mounted, with the mounting coupled to an aiming device which would take account of the tank's irregular motion. He wondered if his Chinese engineers would come up with something; he wasn't hopeful about his own prospects of doing so.

The General did not seem too discouraged by the trial; like most Chinese, he was impressed by noise, and the tank—even without accurate firepower—was satisfyingly noisy. He was in good spirits as they prepared to remount to ride back to the main camp. It was at this point that Simon noticed a black dot against the snow at the far end of the pass, and drew the General's attention to it. It soon resolved itself into a mounted figure. A man on horseback must be of the gentry, and a solitary rider was unusual. They reined in their horses and waited.

As he got nearer, Simon recognized the horseman as a young officer who was second in command of the courier's troop. His horse looked dead beat, and so did he. His face was grey with more than just exhaustion.

The General spoke calmly, but with an underlying grimness: "What news, from the Court of Heaven?"

The man was trembling. "Nothing good, Lord General. Disaster. Death. Destruction."

A second messenger, travelling at a more leisurely pace and accompanied by the customary troop of horsemen, arrived some days later. He presented the General with a silk scroll, yellow-edged to certify it as emanating from the Son of Heaven.

The message it brought was concise and clear.

The Emperor Yuan Chu sent greetings to his loyal general. A new age had dawned which would bring peace, happiness, and prosperity to the Middle Kingdom. The Son of Heaven commanded his loyal servant to return to Li Nan, where he would receive due reward for his exploits against the northern barbarians, and advice as to future conduct. There should be no delay in the performance of this duty.

So the Lord Chancellor had finally pulled off a coup, Simon thought. Taking tea with the General, he said: "What will you do, sire?"

"The faintest breath from the Son of Heaven is a tempest no ordinary mortal can withstand or should wish to."

"Yes, but . . ."

"A humble servant such as I must do his master's bidding, even though he may suspect that the reward he is promised will be that the axeman rather than the torturer should end his life. I command the army of the north, the most powerful army of the Middle Kingdom. No emperor dare risk its loyalty."

Simon was silent. He knew about Chinese fatalism, but this was ridiculous.

The General went on: "But a wise servant makes

sure he knows who his master is. The message is written on yellow-bordered silk and carries the imperial seal. But silks and seals have fallen into unworthy hands before now. For Yuan Chu to have become the Son of Heaven, Cho-tsing must first have gone to join his ancestors."

"Do you think he *is* dead?"

"Those who brought the scroll say he is. But there is an ancient proverb which says that loudly crying the tiger's death does not kill the tiger."

Simon thought of the boy lying in the sun beside the jade-rimmed swimming pool, playing with the chattering monkeys. What had become of them, he wondered? He asked, hoping for reassurance: "He might have escaped?"

"All I know is that I do not know that he is dead. And unless Yuan Chu sends me his head, I shall not choose to believe it. And even if the head is sent, perhaps I shall not recognize it. I swore loyalty to Cho-tsing, and in the spring I shall take my army south, to find him. Or perhaps avenge him."

During the winter, recruiting parties were sent out, and reinforcements arrived in numbers which surprised Simon until he realized the newcomers were collecting substantial enlistment bonuses. It appeared that for years the General had been building up a contingency fund out of military budget surpluses, and Simon wondered if he had perhaps all along been contemplating the possibility of some independent action. He did not think it wise to put the question, but the General provided the hint of an answer one day when they were watching the recruits being drilled.

"They are clumsy," he said, "but they will learn. My officers, who have been well trained for this, will teach them. An army requires three things, Si Mun: good food, good boots, good discipline. With them, we shall win our battle in the spring."

He paused for some moments before continuing.

"And then, if we do not find Cho-tsing living, I shall of necessity be the new Son of Heaven. That is not of my seeking. I would have been content to grow old in the Emperor's service and retire at last to some small mansion with a garden, a fish pond, views of lake and mountain. Instead I shall live in the great palace at Li Nan, surrounded by courtiers and slaves, by concubines and eunuchs, by liars and flatterers. Will you stay with me there, Si Mun, so that I may have one honest man at my side?"

Simon said warily: "I'm not sure I'd be of much use."

"An honest man no use?" The General smiled. "But you are wise to hesitate. A tyrant may think he wants honest advice, but he lies to himself in thinking it. And the Son of Heaven, providing he rules at all, must be a tyrant whether he wills it or not. Celebrate my victory with me in the Crimson Palace; then take your booty back to your Lomani land. Or else one day it may be you who begs the favour of an axeman rather than a torturer."

He smiled again, but the smile was as wintry as the frozen landscape about them. Although he had grown quite to like him, Simon decided that he had just been given very good advice.

Bei W'ih rejoined them a few days before the army began its march south. He said to Simon: "The general ill sometimes confers benefit on the individual—we meet again much sooner than expected. And I hear good report of you and your ironclad steam wagons which crawl like serpents. It is strange, though. Had I been asked which might prove an inventor, it would not have been you I proposed but your friend, B'lad."

"Is there any news of him?"

"No news of B'lad. But Bei Pen sends you greetings."

As he said that, Simon was aware of a tingling warmth, a small exploding shock inside his head, greetings not spoken but communicated, mind to mind. It gave him a feeling of exhilaration, mixed with fear. The possibility of Bei Pen making mental contact, at this distance and after such a time, had never occurred to him. He jerked his head, shaking it from him, and asked: "Are your dragons prepared to fly?"

Bei W'ih smiled comfortably; he had put on weight during the winter.

"They will fly when the time is ripe."

They travelled south as the year brightened, going by easy stages, with the three tanks which had been completed hissing and clanking in the van. They broke down from time to time, but the Chinese manning them were skilled at getting them back into working order. The aiming problem had not been solved, so they had been fitted with catapults which would hurl grenades ahead of them, scattering indiscriminate destruction. In any case, Simon thought, it was the psychological effect of their appearance—as in the case of the elephants Hannibal put into the fighting line against the Romans—which would be most important. They certainly aroused wonder and admiration in the villages and towns through which the army passed.

The populace seemed to be firmly on the General's side, greeting the army with cheers and flowers. They were fortunate with the weather, too; apart from a couple of days of squally rain, it stayed fine. And with recruits continuing to flock in, their progress came to resemble a victory tour. When they pitched camp fifteen miles from Li Nan without having encountered any opposition, Simon speculated on the possibility of Yuan Chu abandoning the capital and fleeing south. But the General dismissed it.

"To yield the Crimson Palace would be to yield all. He must fight. But he has left it too late. Now he must come to us here, in a valley where we hold the western ground and where the wind, at this time of year, is from the west. The dragons will fly strongly above us."

"But in that case might he not just wait in Li Nan? We couldn't stay here indefinitely."

"With an enemy so close to the city, he cannot wait. He would lose dignity beyond endurance. And more and more would abandon him and come to us. He will march soon. Within ten days."

Over the next few days, having time on his hands, Simon explored the area surrounding the camp. In particular, he returned to a village they had just passed through, where they had been greeted with even more enthusiasm than usual. He was recognized as the foreigner who had ridden at the General's side, and made much of. The headman of the village invited him to dinner in his house, and dainties were pressed on him. This was especially pleasant since a lot of the pressing was done by the headman's three teenage daughters.

Simon found himself particularly attracted by the middle one, a tall slender girl called Ki Ti. She was the least pretty and the most reserved, but she had a look at once grave and warm, and haunting eyes. On his third visit to the house, with her sisters temporarily out of earshot, her reserve melted a little. She asked him if he would live in Li Nan after the battle, at the court of the new emperor. He said: "For a time, perhaps. Will you come and visit me there?"

She smiled, shaking her head. She had never travelled farther than another village, three miles away. And no village girl would dare enter the precinct of the Son of Heaven.

"Then I will come back here to visit you."

She shook her head at that, too. He would have insisted, but her sisters returned, giggling, and the moment passed. In a way, he was glad of it. He liked her, but he doubted the reliability of his promise. There would be too many other things to do for him to be serious about coming back here. Finding Brad, for one.

Next day, the General's scouts reported an army leaving Li Nan, and the following morning it was encamped at the valley's eastern end. Simon still found it difficult to believe that the enemy was preparing to launch an attack; they knew even better than the barbarians the power of the dragons of Bei-Kun. But in early afternoon, they came on.

There was the ritual exchange of artillery fire, in which honours seemed fairly even and casualties relatively light. In the succeeding lull, the General said: "Now, Si Mun, we will have your crawling wagons."

The tanks advanced through gaps purposely left in the advance ranks of the army. They looked very impressive, the din of their progress accentuated by the silence which had fallen on the field of battle. It must be quite alarming, Simon thought, to encounter them for the first time. He felt a swell of pride in his own achievement.

At that point, one of the tanks gasped to a halt as it reached the edge of no-man's-land. Halfway across, a second followed suit. That one at least began hurling its grenades at the enemy lines, but the spectacle of two monsters out of the three immobilized clearly extinguished any fear that might have been building up in the ranks of Yuan Chu's men and replaced it with quickly burgeoning confidence. They advanced with a roar, swarming over and bringing to a halt the last tank, and coming on to charge the General's front line.

The reversal had taken place with stunning speed. Simon said: "I'm sorry."

He and the general were standing on a rise of ground which gave a good view of the field. The General shrugged. "It is not important. The dragons are ready to fly."

The kites were low in the sky, but climbed rapidly. The General's luck was holding, Simon thought with relief: although there was a prevailing wind, it might have failed them today, but in fact seemed stronger than usual. He heard a great shout of satisfaction from their own ranks, cries of what sounded like dismay from the others. Now, for both sides, the kites would be starting to turn into dragons—dragons sweeping in disdainful flight above the puny earthbound creatures below. The miracle was happening again; Simon felt he was almost on the verge of seeing it himself. Relentlessly the dragons came on, soaring and swooping in their dance of pomp and power.

This was the moment for the command which would turn the faltering awestruck enemy into a scattering rabble. Simon looked to the General for confirmation but as he did so heard a noise: a faraway grumbling buzz, like the hum of a distant bee. No, two bees—more. The General also heard it and asked: "What sound is that?"

As he spoke, and before they came into view at the end of the valley, Simon recognized it. And, recognizing it, he knew at last where Brad had been these past months, and what he had been up to.

Five of them flew along the valley in ragged formation. As aeroplanes, they were nothing much— small and crude, single-engined. But the point was that they flew and, smashing through the dancing dragons, shattered illusion and left a pathetic reality in their wake. Paper and bamboo strips showered from the sky like confetti as the dragon squadrons collapsed and died. The roar of engines faded as the planes flew on. For a second or two, there was a hush before, with a howl of exultation that rose like a storm, the enemy charged the demoralized lines of the General's forces.

The General did not speak as his army disintegrated before their eyes. Simon said: "I'll get the horses." They were tethered to a tree close by. His, disturbed by the noise of the planes and battle generally, whinnied and reared, and it took him a little time to soothe it. When he had done so, he looked back to see the General with his sword drawn from its sheath.

Simon's immediate thought was that if the General were planning a suicidal counterattack, riding into the ranks of the charging enemy, he was opting out. But that was not the General's intention. He lifted his sword and stared briefly at its gleaming point; Simon saw his lips move, but no sound came out. They were still moving as, without looking down, he pressed the point against his chest and drove it home. He fell forward, slumping across the sword.

There was small doubt that he was dead, and no time anyway for doing anything except getting away; already the tide of the retreating rabble was getting close. Simon quickly mounted and spurred his horse on.

He was not the only horseman galloping westwards; others were showing similar prudence. Behind him, the noise of battle—the cries of fear and triumph—faded and died. He was falling behind the other fleeing officers, probably because he was a much less skilled horseman, but the important thing was that he was getting farther and farther away from the battlefield; there was no particular urgency now.

Ahead of him, a sound emerged and grew, this time immediately identifiable as the planes returning. That was, he was forced to admit, a pretty considerable achievement on Brad's part. He was thinking of Brad as the roar grew louder, and of Li Mei. She must have had a part in the palace revolution, possibly the major one. Then, as the roar increased to a crescendo, he had no thought for anything except controlling his horse. It veered off its course, bucking sideways. He believed he had it under control again, before it bucked still more violently and he parted company with the saddle.

Recovering consciousness, the first thing he was aware of was the stink. He did not need a noisy grunting to tell him what it was: concentrated pig. It was dark, and he was in a confined space, with a wall at his back and something more yielding a few inches in front of him. The grunting came from that direction. He struggled to sit up, pushed against and dislodged a low ceiling. Debris scattered as he got to his feet. Although woozy, he recognized his sur-roundings: the pigsty abutted on a wooden building, a peasant's hut, but one slightly larger than the average—Ki Ti's father's house.

A small child who had been watching ran into the house with a cry, and almost immediately Ki Ti appeared. Simon smiled at her and started to step out of the pigsty's annexe. To his surprise, her own look was not a welcoming one but fearful. Hurrying to him, she pushed him down again, put back the bam-boo screen he had dislodged, and began piling rubbish on top of it. As she did so, she explained: the Emperor's soldiers were everywhere, hunting down the survivors of the rebel army. They had been several times to her father's house, and some were actually quartered in the village. He must lie low, make no sound. She would come to him when darkness fell.

His brief glimpse of the sky had told him it was about the middle of the day, and he had plenty of time to think before the evening. In sending his men to exterminate the remnants of the defeated rebels, Yuan Chu was following immemorial custom. They would be merciless in carrying this out and equally ruthless towards anyone protecting the enemies of the Son of Heaven. One of the villagers must have discovered him after he was thrown by his horse, and told Ki Ti's father. They had carried him back and, knowing their house would be visited and searched, had quickly constructed this camouflaged cell in the pigsty as a place of concealment.

In doing so, they had been fully aware of the appalling risks they ran. Discovery would mean death and destruction, not just for the headman and his family and house, but probably for the entire village. He was staggered by their generosity and courage, and determined not to let them remain in this hazardous situation any longer than was necessary. To leave during daylight would risk exposure for them, as well as himself. He would go when night fell, when Ki Ti returned.

It was a long time before he heard her clearing the rubbish from above his head and, after that, lifting the screen. The night air was marvellously fresh after the stifling stench of pig. He said urgently: "I must go, Ki Ti. At once. I am grateful to you, to everyone, for hiding me, but I cannot endanger you by remaining." He stood up. "I cannot thank you enough. Now I must leave."

She whispered: "Speak low. I have food and water. You cannot go, Si Mun."

"I must."

"The Emperor's troops are everywhere. They will catch you when day comes, if not sooner."

"I'll take a chance on that."

"All day, for miles around, they have been finding and killing. If anyone should be caught coming from here, they will guess he has been helped. They will question you, and it will be a hard questioning." She paused. "The ones who came here used harsh words. They have heard that the people in these parts welcomed the army from the north."

He knew what she meant: they were spoiling to make an example of some village, and she could not trust him, under torture, not to give them away. Nor, for that matter, could he. He was silent.

She said: "Eat and drink. I must not stay long."

He tried for a time to keep track of the days, but eventually lost count. He was allowed to stretch his legs a little at night, with village children keeping watch—they would boom like a crane, he was told, if a stranger approached.

There was a terrifying incident a couple of days

after he was first hidden when soldiers did come, not only to the house but to the pigsty. They were requisitioning the pigs, and he lay petrified while someone wrestled a reluctant pig out of the sty, a few inches from his head. But the camouflage worked, and he listened to them driving the pigs away down the hill. Life was less smelly after that, but lonelier: his grunting oinking neighbours had been company.

Ki Ti came every night, but their conversation was limited by their awareness of the soldiers almost within earshot. She apologized for the meagreness of the food she brought—it was not just pigs which had been taken by the occupying troops. Then one day she came when it was still light, her face showing joy and relief. The soldiers had left the village early in the morning; the imperial army was marching back to Li Nan.

That night, he ate with the rest of the family, in the headman's house. The meal included delicacies which, like he himself, had been carefully concealed, and even wine. At the end, he made a kind of speech, thanking them, or trying to. Anything he said must, he knew, be inadequate.

Ki Ti's father spoke in reply. The great ones

came and went, flourished and fell. Oppression continued, whichever emperor ruled. The humble ones were obliged to endure it as best they could. But there were good things in life beyond a tyrant's reach: the warming sun, the nourishing land, the company of friends. They had been honoured to have their friend, Si Mun, as a guest. He could depart now, without danger. Or, if he wished, stay with them.

They were good people; he could not expect to find better anywhere. It would not be a bad life, sharing their work and pleasure through the seasons and years. He saw Ki Ti watching him, her dark eyes solemn. Not just not bad, but good, in so many ways. And yet, understanding the value of what was offered, he could not accept it. There were things to settle, answers to find, doubts to resolve.

He said to Ki Ti's father: "The honour you do me is as great as the aid you have given me. If I could stay, I would; but I must go."

It was chill and misty in the foothills, and this time when he came out onto the plateau the mist still clung. The granite walls of the bonzery, which had once sparkled in sunlight, were grey and gloomy.

He found no one inside the building, but that was not particularly surprising: the priests could be working in the fields or in the pagoda. As he went through to the terrace, though, he saw someone, partly hidden by a trail of ivy, looking out.

The figure, conscious of his approach, turned towards him. Even though he still could not distinguish who it was, he had a sense of familiarity, of recognition. Bei Pen, he guessed, half dreading, half wanting the voice inside his head.

But it was Brad.

THEY WALKED PAST PLOTS OF DEAD OR dying crops. When Simon referred to this, Brad shrugged.

"The weather's turned bad."

The afternoon was grey and cold; a wind keened in from the escarpment, knife-edged.

"For any particular reason?"

"A lot of the priests have gone. And I suppose the ones still here have lost heart."

"You mean, they were using some kind of combined mental force to control the weather, and that's cracked up?"

"Something like that."

They went past the greenhouse with the peaches. Those fruits still on the branch were withered, the glossy green leaves crumpled and blackened by frost. They were walking with no apparent aim, but Simon suddenly realized they had come to the hollow where the confrontation between Bei Pen and Li Mei had taken place. Fish still swam in the pool, but the willow had cast most of its spears onto the water. Unable to restrain himself any longer, he asked abruptly: "What did happen—about Li Mei?"

"I don't know what's happened."

It wasn't an answer. Simon said: "The aeroplanes were your idea."

It came out more accusingly than he had intended, but Brad didn't seem to mind. He said, in simple explanation: "The dragons were the big problem, of course. She had the power to put her own up, but it would only have equalled things out. If that. She couldn't be sure of getting the windward station. But it all depended on illusion, so if there was some way the illusion could be shattered . . . She saw the point in aircraft right away." He paused, and added dispassionately: "She has a good brain."

"And you?"

"Well, it wasn't . . ."

"I wasn't talking about your terrific brain. *Your* illusion, about Li Mei. What shattered that?"

Brad said slowly: "I saw her as she really was."

"As I recall, that happened right here. Bei Pen forced you to see it. But I thought you'd decided you preferred the illusion to the reality."

"I don't mean physical appearance. Her real self. I could understand her hating Bei Pen after what he'd done to her, in front of us. I wasn't too bothered by her being determined to get back at him, either. She had no hope of doing anything here, but the imperial court was different. She went to work on Yuan Chu. I still wasn't bothered. There have been plenty of palace revolutions in China in the past, and there'll be plenty more to come."

"I shouldn't think they're ever very pleasant for the poor devils caught up in them."

"No. Neither was the Christian revolution against the Roman emperor—nor a lot of other things that have happened since the fireball." He was silent a moment. "But you're right. I didn't realize it at the time, but I did later. It wasn't the actual fighting, which was over quickly, but what happened after. Yuan Chu ordered a general massacre—not just of soldiers and officials, but the women as well. I was told he strangled the Dowager Empress with his own hands."

"And . . . Cho-tsing?"

In a wooden voice, Brad said: "I thought being with Li Mei and helping her to help Yuan Chu gave me a right to ask favours. I pointed out Cho-tsing was just a boy and had never wanted to be emperor. Yuan Chu said that made no difference, because people might use him. He had to be killed, and since others might claim he was still alive and start revolts in his name, he must die publicly, in the market square of Li Nan. And so that the citizenry should properly mark and remember it, the execution would last from dawn until dusk."

Simon was engulfed by a wave of sickness and anger. He had long given up hope that Cho-tsing could have survived, but he had not imagined this sort of horror. He had been so gentle; Simon remembered the look on his face when one of his monkeys was ill. He had an impulse to say to Brad: "You went chasing after your illusion, and look what

that did to Cho-tsing—not in illusion, but for real."
But he knew there was nothing he could say to Brad
which Brad had not said already to himself.

He stayed silent as Brad went on: "That's when I
went to Li Mei. I didn't anticipate any real difficulty.
Yuan Chu might be emperor, but it was Li Mei who
had put him on the throne, and he needed her help
against a possible counterrevolution by people like
your general. We'd planned the planes, but Yuan
Chu didn't have them yet. He depended on her, and
she could put pressure on.

"I couldn't believe it when she refused to do anything. I told her Cho-tsing was my friend, but she
wasn't interested. I said, even apart from that, I wasn't
going to stand for anything so barbaric and sadistic—
no civilized person could. She looked at me as though
I were a child, or an insect. So I pleaded with her . . .
in the end, I cried. She smiled. That was the real ugli-
ness, not what Bei Pen showed me.

"So then I got angry. I even went for her, with
some crazy idea of physically forcing her to save
him. What a laugh that was. Her voice came inside
my head, and I couldn't speak—couldn't move. She
called soldiers. I expected her to have me killed, and

didn't mind, but they put me in a cell instead. I suppose even though she'd got the planes, she reckoned I might still be of some use. I was in the dungeon a long time: all through the winter. I had plenty of time to think, and work things out. The roots of her madness probably went a long way back, before Bei-Kun's other disciple, her brother, died. But that precipitated things. She feared death, hated the aged body which she could not disguise from herself, had this insane urge to destroy. Destruction for her became the only thing worth living for. And all I was was a useful tool."

The last words were said with bitterness and self-contempt. There was a silence.

Simon asked: "How did you escape?"

"There was a big celebration when news of the victory reached the city. All the guards were drunk. Getting out wasn't all that difficult, and I headed here. One place seemed as good as another, or as bad."

Simon said: "What do we do now?"

Brad shrugged. "I haven't thought. I guessed it was possible you might turn up. Not all that likely, but possible. I didn't plan any further."

"Well, maybe we'd better start planning. One place may be as bad as another, but I have a feeling this one could be worse than most with Li Mei on the rampage."

Only about a dozen priests appeared for the midday meal, which consisted chiefly of boiled rice. Towards the end, they were joined by Bei Pen. Simon thought he might ask questions about recent events, but he did not. In the end, Simon brought up the subject of the battle himself. He found himself taking satisfaction in describing how the aeroplanes had torn the dragons into shreds.

He realized he was trying to provoke Bei Pen, and realized too the unfairness of it. The system of peace and order which had stemmed from the Laws of Bei-Kun had been better than most. It was tolerably certain any succeeding situation was going to be a lot worse than the old. But he could not help himself.

"They drifted down out of the sky like scraps of paper," he said. "But that's all they were, weren't they? Just scraps of paper."

The other priests had left. Bei Pen said: "Illusion

prevails until doubt enters. Then illusion is no more than a thicket of gossamer, and doubt is a charging bull."

"Which amounts to saying it's all fake really, all a pretence. You could do fantastic things like growing peaches on top of a mountain, controlling weather, but they only worked as long as you could keep the mental ranks solid behind you. The moment your grip on that weakened, everything started to collapse."

Brad suddenly looked up. "When you had the showdown with Li Mei, did you have any idea what might come of it?"

"Not might come, but must. I knew it much earlier than that. From the moment two boys came through the fireball from another world into this one."

"And yet you had us brought here from Li Nan!"

"That which must happen, will happen. But to see the future is not to know the ways of reaching it, which are infinite. And I was curious."

Simon demanded: "Can you see our futures?"

"I have not looked."

"Then will you?"

Bei Pen shook his head. "No."

Simon's mind was full of confused resentments and anger. He felt the voice come into his head, the other mind touch his. "Be at peace." Resentment flared into fury, and he flashed back defiance: "Get out!"

The voice went but, strangely, in going took his anger with it. He did not know, and never would, whether or not Bei Pen could have forced his will if he had chosen to; but he knew with certainty that it was something which would never happen. His freedom of will was as precious to Bei Pen as to himself. This was someone he could trust, now and always. The revelation which followed was a proof of that, trusting him as he trusted. He looked and saw not the Bei Pen he thought he knew, but the real man—old, so old, withered and bent not by decades but by centuries.

He saw something else and cried out: "You're not Chinese!"

"No," Bei Pen said. "I was not born in this land, Si Mun. I was born in yours."

He had been born in England, in the year 1967 from the founding of Rome. He had grown up in a Christian community and had become a Christian priest. Then, as a young man, he was befriended by the Roman governor of the Britannic Isles, a man who later succeeded to the purple and took him with him to Rome.

It had been a pleasant existence, but gradually he came to find the pleasantness cloying and unsatisfactory. There were questions, about life, about the universe, which he did not find easy to pursue in the complacent flippant atmosphere of the imperial capital. It was then he met a traveller from the east, who told him of the wonders of the Middle Kingdom.

So he left Rome and made the long and difficult journey to the land of the Chinese. There he studied both their new inventions and the wisdom of the sages: Confucius, the Buddha, Lao-tzu. Out of this study, after many years, he formed the Laws.

Brad, who had been listening closely, said: "Did you say 1967 from the founding of the city? In our world, we dated from the birth of Christ, which happened in the Roman year 753. So in our world you would have been born in A.D. 1214. In Somerset, England? Near Ilchester?"

"I do not know how you know it, but yes. Close by the town of Ilchester."

"So it does fit!"

"Everything fits," Bei Pen said, "providing one knows the pattern."

"Fits?" Simon asked. "What fits?"

"The Laws of Bei-Kun and the fireball. They're part of the same thing."

"Are you saying the fireball was responsible for Bei-Kun being born in Somerset? That's crazy."

Brad's face had the happy look which came when he had worked out a particularly tough problem.

"He was a genius—you could say, a super genius. They called him Doctor Mirabilis, the Wonderful Teacher. He studied everything: alchemy, mechanics, the black arts. He was said to have made a bronze head, which spoke three times. It said "Time is," then "Time was," finally "Time's past," and burst into smithereens. That sounds a bit farfetched, but he did leave records suggesting some interesting experiments—filling a balloon made of thin sheet copper with what he called liquid fire so that it would float, for instance; and making a flying machine with flapping wings.

"But he didn't get on too well with the church authorities. They probably didn't like the black arts business. He was kept in close confinement for ten years. Then another pope pardoned him, but he'd learned his lesson. He kept a low profile after that."

Brad looked at Bei Pen. "At least, that's what happened in our world. But things were different in this one. Here the church didn't have any power to discipline him. And he found nothing in Rome to sharpen his wits on. So he travelled to China which, in the thirteenth century, was full of ideas and new developments. The combination of that with a Western super-genius produced the Laws. They were called after him. The Laws of Bei-Kun. Bacon—Roger Bacon!"

"That was my name," Bei Pen said. "It is a long time since I heard it spoken. And it is true that I have learned many things, over many lifetimes. Come, there are things to show you."

The portico leading to the pagoda made sense now—an echo of the Roman world that Bei-Kun, Bacon, had abandoned. Inside it was bare and mono-chrome: ceiling, walls, and floor in shades of blue which deepened in hue from top to bottom. Stairs led both up and down; as they went down, the blue deepened still further. Oil lamps flickered behind blue glass.

The basement was larger in area than the ground floor, with curved outer walls. It was as though the upper part of the building was a flower, and they were inside the bulb. A velvet curtain was so darkly blue that at first it seemed black. Bei Pen parted it and beckoned them to follow him through.

Simon started to move, then stopped, halted by a feeling of dread and awe that was like a heavy weight. The wordless voice spoke—"There is nothing to fear." Brad, too, had halted. Simon took his arm and led him through the curtain.

They were in a bare blue room, lit by four blue lamps. They squatted on rugs on the polished wooden floor, equidistant from one another on the periphery of a circle, looking inwards. Silence pressed down, and Simon was aware of his own ragged breath. Although nothing had been said, he knew he must not move, not even turn an eye. Out of the stillness and emptiness in front of him, he was aware of something being born.

It came as a kaleidoscope of images, filling the centre of the room but shifting so fast that they were no more than fleeting glimpses in a chaotic blur. Gradually the images became clearer, longer lasting. He was able to distinguish familiar things: landscapes, cities, animals and birds, people. . . . Some scenes came and went, beneath changing skies. He saw a boat very like the *Stella Africanus*, a bearded face that could be Bos. . . .

Now he was looking into a room. He knew it well—the clock on the wall, the curtains stirring in a breeze, the bronze fox crouching beside the open fire. He had stroked its head when he was scarcely able to walk. There had been a fireguard then, with firelight glowing through it.

And he knew the figure in the Windsor chair, listening to a play on the radio as he had often watched her do. She looked older, more tired, and her hair was whiter. He saw where her gaze rested: on a picture on the mantelshelf in a Victorian silver frame, a photograph of himself.

The scene faded. He wanted to call it back, but the emptiness swallowed it from within. Another scene took shape.

There was no fire in this room. It was barer and larger, and the painting on the wall was a violent abstract which would have made his grandmother shake her head in disapproval. Sunlight flooded in from a verandah, and there was a faraway snore of surf. A deeply tanned man in Bermuda shorts knelt on a Mexican rug. He looked a bit like Brad did when something was absorbing him. He was playing with a child just starting to walk, a boy.

That scene went in turn, and Bei Pen stood up. They followed him through the curtain, up the stairs and out of the pagoda. The wind seemed colder and carried darts of rain.

Standing beneath the portico, Simón said: "More illusions?"

Bei Pen shook his head. "Those places are as real as this."

"But they're on the other side of the fireball! So even if they aren't illusions, they might as well be. Why show them to us?"

"When you found the fireball, you stumbled by accident on a manifestation of something which was unravelled here over long years of study. The universe is infinite, and there is an infinity of universes, existing side by side, like threads in a limitless carpet. Rarely, very rarely, two threads may touch, and fray. The fireball was such a fraying. An accident—if anything in the universe is accidental—and one which would not repeat itself in aeons. If ever. But that does not mean the way back is barred to you. By the power of first mind, which is modelled on the Mind that created and keeps in being everything that is, threads can be brought together. You can be returned to your own world, if that is what you wish."

Bei Pen left them and went back in to the pagoda. Simon felt dazed. It took time for the realization of what they had been told to penetrate fully, but when it did he had no doubts. Bei Pen would not lie to him or deceive him. They could return to the world on the other side of the fireball. He said to Brad: "He can do it, if he says he can. I'm sure of it. He's giving us time to make our minds up, but there's no need for that, is there? Let's go right in and tell him yes."

Brad was staring at the sky above the foothills. When Simon started to speak again, Brad shushed him. He was listening to something, and in a moment Simon picked it out himself: the distant growl of an engine.

Simon said incredulously: "A plane?"

Soon they could see a dot in the sky. Other dots emerged from cloud to join it, and the growling grew louder. Simon counted four, flying in rough line formation. He said: "There are no dragons here, and nowhere they could land. So what's it in aid of?"

They came on slowly. This world had a long way to go before it reached the stage of Harriers and Phantoms. Slowly, but steadily . . .

The first bomb dropped a long way short, as did the second; but the third and fourth landed near the edge of the plateau. The boys hit the ground and remained there while the brief but violent bombardment lasted. The blast from one impact struck Simon's back like a giant's flail. Then the roar of engines dwindled, and they got to their feet and looked around.

The most obvious result of the raid was a crashed plane, forty or fifty yards away. It was still burning fiercely: the scorched figure of the pilot sat upright in a tangle of wires from which the bamboo struts had burnt away. He must have misjudged his altitude.

Looking away, Simon saw a bomb crater in a

field, a flattened greenhouse, a wrecked dormitory hut. He said to Brad: "Was it worth it? One plane down, at least—very possibly more. I wouldn't fancy flying over those mountains on a single engine. In return for trivial damage like this."

"The amount of damage isn't important, is it? Getting here was enough—letting loose another raging bull in the gossamer thicket of illusion. Most of the rest of the priests will leave now, maybe all except Bei Pen. And the weather will get worse. We could be knee-deep in snow by tomorrow morning."

"You think it's getting near the end?"

"It's a funny thing, isn't it?" Brad said. "That there should be such incredible mental power, and that it should be so vulnerable. Yet I suppose it's all in conformity with the law of suggestion. Maybe the pagoda could hold out for a while—that's where the power must be strongest—but eventually that will go, too."

"The important thing is that *we* can go. And I suggest we don't waste much time about it."

There was a pause, before Brad said: "I'm not going back."

Simon stared at him. "Are you mad? We're stuck

on top of a mountain which you reckon will be hit by blizzards within hours, in the middle of a hostile continent, with complexions that stick out like cream on custard, and with you in particular wanted dead or alive—preferably alive so that Li Mei can take her time over the death bit. . . . You do realize that, don't you? You're not still hooked on her?"

Brad said: "I didn't mean I want to stay here. He told us: there's an infinity of worlds. If he can put us back in the one we came from, he can put me in some other."

"Which could be a lot worse than the one we're in right now. Have sense."

"I'll take a chance on it."

Simon said bitterly: "Just because your dad's remarried and has another son!"

"Unworthy of you, chum." Brad's tone was surprisingly mild, though. "It doesn't matter. You go back to Gran. I'm moving on."

Simon followed Brad, fuming. There was, he knew, no point in pursuing the argument; he had come to know the strength of Brad's obstinacy during their three years of adventuring. He thought of the night of the Indian feast, just before the Chinese slavers arrived, when he had accused himself of weakness of character for following Brad's whims. This was one whim he certainly wasn't going to follow. He had vowed then, not for a moment believing it to be possible, that if they ever got back to their own world, he would cheerfully wave him good-bye. Well, he was ready to wave good-bye right now. He was going to go back, whatever crazy notion Brad might have.

They found Bei Pen in the lower room. He said: "You have decided."

It wasn't a question.

Brad said: "Simon's going back. I'd rather try a different probability world. Can that be done?"

Bei Pen said: "Think of a spinning wheel, with a million times a million spokes. One of them is the place from which you started; if I set you loose from this world, there is that within your soul which will take you to it, as a pigeon, over great distances, returns to its box."

So that was that, Simon thought with relief. Brad's latest whim just wouldn't work.

Bei Pen paused, and went on: "But if, having been loosed, your mind should choose to reject its proper destination, it has the power to do so. You will come to rest in some other plane."

Brad nodded. "Good."

"Is it good? There will be no way of directing where you come to rest. The possibilities are infinite. Not just of worlds in which some great person died or did not die. There are worlds in which men are savages still, lacking even such primitive skills as that of making fire—worlds in which man never existed, in which reptiles taller than trees stalk one another—worlds in which life never even began. . . . There is no knowing what you will find. It may well be death."

Brad gave it perhaps a second's thought.

"Okay. I'll take my chances."

"May the Great Spirit go with you." Bei Pen turned to Simon. "And you will go home?"

It came to him with the weight almost of a blow that going home meant parting from Bei Pen as well as Brad, but before he had time to think about it, their minds were joined again. In that joining, he was made acquainted with many things: unutterable weariness, a deep longing for rest and peace, and the certainty that peace would not be long delayed. He knew too that though this was the last time their minds would meet, the echo would stay and sustain him.

So he thought instead of pushing open a door to see a table laid for tea, hearing the kettle's song, smelling bread baking in the kitchen. What a fool Brad was, a stupid and irresponsible fool! He attempted to catch his eye, with one last hope of having him see reason, but Brad refused it.

And what an even bigger fool he was himself.

"No," he said. "I've changed my mind. I'm going with him."

Turn the page for a peek at another
adventure series by John Christopher.

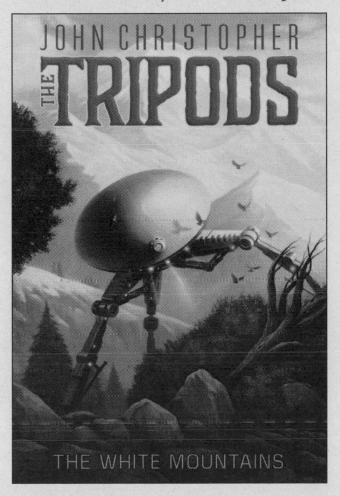

JOHN CHRISTOPHER

THE TRIPODS

THE WHITE MOUNTAINS

APART FROM THE ONE IN THE CHURCH TOWER, there were five clocks in the village that kept reasonable time, and my father owned one of them. It stood on the mantelpiece in the parlor, and every night before he went to bed he took the key from a vase, and wound it up. Once a year the clockman came from Winchester, on an old jogging packhorse, to clean and oil it and put it right. Afterward he would drink camomile tea with my mother, and tell her the news of the city and what he had learned in the villages through which he had passed. My father, if he were not busy milling, would stalk out at this time, with some contemptuous remark about gossip; but later, in the evening, I would hear my mother passing the stories on to him. He did not show much enthusiasm, but he listened to them.

My father's great treasure, though, was not the clock, but the Watch. This, a miniature clock with a dial less than an inch across and a circlet permitting it to be worn on the wrist, was kept in a locked drawer of his desk; and only brought out to be worn on ceremonial occasions, like Harvest Festival, or a Capping. The clockman was only allowed to see to it every third year, and at such times my father stood by, watching him as he worked. There was no other Watch in the village, nor in any of the villages round about. The clockman said there were a number in Winchester, but none as fine as this. I wondered if he said it to please my father, who certainly showed pleasure in the hearing, but I believe it truly was of very good workmanship. The body of the Watch was of a steel much superior to anything they could make at the forge in Alton, and the works inside were a wonder of intricacy and skill. On the front was printed "Anti-magnetique Incabloc," which we supposed must have been the name of the craftsman who made it in olden times.

The clockman had visited us the week before, and I had been permitted to look on for a time while he cleaned and oiled the Watch. The sight fascinated me, and after he had gone I found my thoughts running continually on this treasure, now locked away again in its drawer. I was, of course, forbidden to touch my father's desk and the notion of opening a locked drawer in it should have been unthinkable. Nonetheless, the idea persisted. And after a day or two, I admitted to myself that it was only the fear of being caught that prevented me.

On Saturday morning, I found myself alone in the house. My father was in the mill room, grinding, and the servants—even Molly who normally did not leave the house during the day—had been brought in to help. My mother was out visiting old Mrs. Ash, who was sick, and would be gone an hour at least. I had finished my homework, and there was nothing to stop my going out into the bright May morning and finding Jack. But what completely filled my mind was the thought that I had this opportunity to look at the Watch, with small chance of detection.

The key, I had observed, was kept with the other keys in a small box beside my father's bed. There were four, and the third one opened the drawer. I took out the Watch, and gazed at it. It was not going, but I knew one wound it and set the hands by means of the small knob at one side. If I were to wind it only a couple of turns it would run down quite soon—just in case my father decided to look at it later in the day. I did this, and listened to its quiet rhythmic ticking. Then I set the hands by the clock. After that it only remained for me to slip it on my wrist. Even notched to the first hole, the leather strap was loose; but I was wearing the Watch.

Having achieved what I had thought was an ultimate ambition, I found, as I think is often the case, that there remained something more. To wear it was a triumph, but to be seen wearing it . . . I had told my cousin, Jack Leeper, that I would meet him that morning, in the old ruins at the end of the village. Jack, who was nearly a year older than myself and due to be presented at the next Capping, was the person, next to my parents, that I most admired. To take the Watch out of the house was to add enormity to disobedience, but having already gone so far, it was easier to contemplate it. My mind made up, I was determined to waste none of the precious time I had. I opened the front door, stuck the hand with the Watch deep into my trouser pocket, and ran off down the street.

The village lay at a crossroads, with the road in which our house stood running alongside the river (this giving power for the mill, of course) and the second road crossing it at the ford. Beside the ford stood a small wooden bridge for foot travelers, and I pelted across, noticing that the river was higher than usual from the spring rains. My Aunt Lucy was approaching the bridge as I left it at the far end. She called a greeting to me, and I called back, having first taken care to veer to the other side of the road. The baker's shop was there, with trays of buns and cakes set out, and it was reasonable that I should be heading that way: I had a couple of pennies in my pocket. But I ran on past it, and did not slacken to a walk until I had reached the point where the houses thinned out and at last ended.

The ruins were a hundred yards farther on. On

one side of the road lay Spiller's meadow, with cows grazing, but on my side there was a thorn hedge, and a potato field beyond. I passed a gap in the hedge, not looking in my concentration on what I was going to show Jack, and was startled a moment later by a shout from behind me. I recognized the voice as Henry Parker's.

Henry, like Jack, was a cousin of mine—my name is Will Parker—but, unlike Jack, no friend. (I had several cousins in the village: people did not usually travel far to marry.) He was a month younger than I, but taller and heavier, and we had hated each other as long as I could remember. When it came to fighting, as it very often did, I was outmatched physically, and had to rely on agility and quickness if I were not going to be beaten. From Jack I had learned some skill in wrestling which, in the past year, had enabled me to hold my own more, and in our last encounter I had thrown him heavily enough to wind him and leave him gasping for breath. But for wrestling one needed the use of both hands. I thrust my left hand deeper into the pocket and, not answering his call, ran on toward the ruins.

He was closer than I had thought, though, and he pounded after me, yelling threats. I put a spurt on, looked back to see how much of a lead I had, and found myself slipping on a patch of mud. (Cobbles were laid inside the village, but out here the road was in its usual poor condition, aggravated by the rains.) I fought desperately to keep my footing, but would not, until it was too late, bring out my other hand to help balance myself. As a result, I went slithering and sprawling and finally fell. Before I could recover, Henry was kneeling across me, holding the back of my head with his hand and pushing my face down into the mud.

This activity would normally have kept him happy for some time, but he found something of greater interest. I had instinctively used both hands to protect myself as I fell, and he saw the Watch on my wrist. In a moment he had wrenched it off, and stood up to examine it. I scrambled to my feet, and made a grab, but he held it easily above his head and out of my reach.

I said, panting, "Give that back!"

"It's not yours," he said. "It's your father's."

I was in agony in case the Watch had been damaged, broken maybe, in my fall, but even so I attempted to get my leg between his, to drop him. He parried, and, stepping back, said,

"Keep your distance." He braced himself, as though preparing to throw a stone. "Or I'll see how far I can fling it."

"If you do," I said, "you'll get a whipping for it."

There was a grin on his fleshy face. "So will you. And your father lays on heavier than mine does. I'll tell you what: I'll borrow it for a while. Maybe I'll let you have it back this afternoon. Or tomorrow."

"Someone will see you with it."

He grinned again. "I'll risk that."

I made a grab at him. I had decided that he was bluffing about throwing it away. I almost got him off balance, but not quite. We swayed and struggled, and then crashed together and rolled down into the ditch by the side of the road. There was some water in it, but we went on fighting, even after a voice challenged us from above. Jack—for it was he who had called to us to get up—had to come down and pull us apart by force. This was not difficult for him. He was as big as Henry, and tremendously strong also. He dragged us back up to the road, got to the root of the matter, took the Watch off Henry, and dismissed him with a clip across the back of the neck.

I said tearfully, "Is it all right?"

"I think so." He examined it, and handed it to me. "But you were a fool to bring it out."

"I wanted to show it to you."

"Not worth it," he said briefly. "Anyway, we'd better see about getting it back. I'll lend a hand."

Jack had always been around to lend a hand, as long as I could remember. It was strange, I thought, as we walked toward the village, that in just over a week's time I would be on my own. The Capping would have taken place, and Jack would be a boy no longer.

Jack stood guard while I put the Watch back and returned the drawer key to the place where I had found it. I changed my wet and dirty trousers and shirt, and we retraced our steps to the ruins. No one knew what these buildings had once been, and I think one of the things that attracted us was a sign, printed on a chipped and rusted metal plate:

DANGER

6,600 VOLTS

We had no idea what Volts had been, but the notion of danger, however far away and long ago, was exciting. There was more lettering, but for the most part the rust had destroyed it. LECT CITY: we wondered if that were the city it had come from.

Farther along was the den Jack had made. One approached it through a crumbling arch; inside it was dry, and there was a place to build a fire. Jack had made one before coming out to look for me, and had skinned, cleaned, and skewered a rabbit ready for us to grill. There would be food in plenty at home— the midday meal on a Saturday was always lavish— but this did not prevent my looking forward greedily to roast rabbit with potatoes baked in the embers of the fire. Nor would it stop me doing justice to the steak pie my mother had in the oven. Although on the small side, I had a good appetite.

We watched and smelled the rabbit cooking in companionable silence. We could get on very well together without much conversation, though normally I had a ready tongue. Too ready, perhaps—I knew that a lot of the trouble with Henry arose because I could not avoid trying to get a rise out of him whenever possible.

Jack was not much of a talker under any circumstances, but to my surprise, after a time he broke the silence. His talk was inconsequential at first, chatter about events that had taken place in the village, but I had the feeling that he was trying to get around to something else, something more important. Then he stopped, stared in silence for a second or two at the crisping carcass, and said,

"This place will be yours, after the Capping."

It was difficult to know what to say. I suppose if I had thought about it at all, I would have expected that he would pass the den on to me, but I had not thought about it. One did not think much about things connected with the Cappings, and certainly did not talk about them. For Jack, of all people, to do so was surprising, but what he said next was more surprising still.

"In a way," he said, "I almost hope it doesn't work. I'm not sure I wouldn't rather be a Vagrant."

I should say something about the Vagrants. Every village generally had a few—at that time there were four in ours, as far as I knew—but the number was constantly changing as some moved off and others took their place. They occasionally did a little work, but whether they did or not the village supported them. They lived in the Vagrant House, which in our case stood on the corner where the two roads crossed and was larger than all but a handful of houses (my father's being one). It could easily have accommodated a dozen Vagrants, and there had been times when there had been almost that many there. Food was supplied to them—it was not luxurious, but adequate—and a servant looked after the place. Other servants were sent to lend a hand when the House filled up.

What was known, though not discussed, was that the Vagrants were people for whom the Capping had proved a failure. They had Caps, as normal people did, but they were not working properly. If this were going to happen, it usually showed itself in the first day or two following a Capping: the person who had been Capped showed distress, which increased as the days went by, turning at last into a fever of the brain. In this state, they were clearly in much pain. Fortunately the crisis did not last long; fortunately also, it happened only rarely. The great majority of Cappings were entirely successful. I suppose only about one in twenty produced a Vagrant.

When he was well again, the Vagrant would start his wanderings. He, or she; because it happened occasionally with girls, although much more rarely. Whether it was because they saw themselves as being outside the community of normal people, or because the fever had left a permanent restlessness in them, I did not know. But off they would go and wander through the land, stopping a day here, as long as a month there, but always moving on. Their minds, certainly, had been affected. None of them could settle to a train of thought for long, and many had visions, and did strange things.

They were taken for granted, and looked after, but, like the Cappings, not much talked about. Children, generally, viewed them with suspicion and avoided them. They, for their part, mostly seemed melancholy, and did not talk much, even to each other. It was a great shock to hear Jack say he half wished to be a Vagrant, and I did not know how to answer him. But he did not seem to need a response. He said, "The Watch—do you ever think what it must have been like in the days when things like that were made?"

I had, from time to time, but it was another subject on which speculation was not encouraged, and Jack had never talked in this way before. I said, "Before the Tripods?"

"Yes."

"Well, we know it was the Black Age. There were too many people, and not enough food, so that people starved, and fought each other, and there were all kinds of sicknesses, and . . ."

"And things like the Watch were made—by men, not the Tripods."

"We don't know that."

"Do you remember," he asked, "four years ago, when I went to stay with my Aunt Matilda?"

I remembered. She was his aunt, not mine, even

though we were cousins: she had married a foreigner. Jack said, "She lives at Bishopstoke, on the other side of Winchester. I went out one day, walking, and I came to the sea. There were the ruins of a city that must have been twenty times as big as Winchester."

I knew of the ruined great-cities of the ancients, of course. But these, too, were little talked of, and then with disapproval and a shade of dread. No one would dream of going near them. It was disquieting even to think of looking at one, as Jack had done. I said, "Those were the cities where all the murdering and sickness were."

"So we are told. But I saw something there. It was the hulk of a ship, rusting away so that in places you could see right through it. And it was bigger than the village. Much bigger."

I fell silent. I was trying to imagine it, to see it in my mind as he had seen it in reality. But my mind could not accept it.

Jack said, "And that was built by men. Before the Tripods came."

Again I was at a loss for words. In the end, I said lamely, "People are happy now."

Jack turned the rabbit on the spit. After a while, he said, "Yes. I suppose you're right."

The weather stayed fine until Capping Day. From morning till night people worked in the fields, cutting the grass for hay. There had been so much rain earlier that it stood high and luxuriant, a promise of good winter fodder. The Day itself, of course, was a holiday. After breakfast, we went to church, and the parson preached on the rights and duties of manhood, into which Jack was to enter. Not of womanhood, because there was no girl to be Capped. Jack, in fact, stood alone, dressed in the white tunic which was prescribed. I looked at him, wondering how he was feeling, but whatever his emotions were, he did not show them.

Not even when, the service over, we stood out in the street in front of the church, waiting for the Tripod. The bells were ringing the Capping Peal, but apart from that all was quiet. No one talked or whispered or smiled. It was, we knew, a great experience for everyone who had been Capped. Even the Vagrants came and stood in the same rapt silence.

But for us children, the time lagged desperately. And for Jack, apart from everyone, in the middle of the street? I felt for the first time a shiver of fear, in the realization that at the next Capping I would be standing there. I would not be alone, of course, because Henry was to be presented with me. There was not much consolation in that thought.

At last we heard, above the clang of bells, the deep staccato booming in the distance, and there was a kind of sigh from everyone. The booming came nearer and then, suddenly, we could see it over the roofs of the houses to the south: the great hemisphere of gleaming metal rocking through the air above the three articulated legs, several times as high as the church. Its shadow came before it, and fell on us when it halted, two of its legs astride the river and the mill. We waited, and I was shivering in earnest now, unable to halt the tremors that ran through my body.

Sir Geoffrey, the Lord of our Manor, stepped forward and made a small stiff bow in the direction of the Tripod; he was an old man, and could not bend much nor easily. And so one of the enormous burnished tentacles came down, gently and precisely, and its tip curled about Jack's waist, and it lifted him up, up, to where a hole opened like a mouth in the hemisphere, and swallowed him.

In the afternoon there were games, and people moved about the village, visiting, laughing, and talking, and the young men and women who were unmarried strolled together in the fields. Then, in the evening, there was the Feast, with tables set up in the street since the weather held fair, and the smell of roast beef mixing with the smells of beer and cider and lemonade, and all kinds of cakes and puddings. Lamps were hung outside the houses; in the dusk they would be lit, and glow like yellow blossoms along the street. But before the Feast started, Jack was brought back to us.

There was the distant booming first, and the quietness and waiting, and the tread of the gigantic feet, shaking the earth. The Tripod halted as before, and the mouth opened in the side of the hemisphere, and then the tentacle swept down and carefully set Jack by the place which had been left for him at

Sir Geoffrey's right hand. I was a long way away, with the children at the far end, but I could see him clearly. He looked pale, but otherwise his face did not seem any different. The difference was in his white shaved head, on which the darker metal tracery of the Cap stood out like a spider's web. His hair would soon grow again, over and around the metal, and, with thick black hair such as he had, in a few months the Cap would be almost unnoticeable. But it would be there all the same, a part of him now till the day he died.

This, though, was the moment of rejoicing and making merry. He was a man, and tomorrow would do a man's work and get a man's pay. They cut the choicest fillet of beef and brought it to him, with a frothing tankard of ale, and Sir Geoffrey toasted his health and fortune. I forgot my earlier fears, and envied him, and thought how next year I would be there, a man myself.

I did not see Jack the next day, but the day after that we met when, having finished my homework, I was on my way to the den. He was with four or five other men, coming back from the fields. I called him, and he smiled and, after a moment's hesitation, let the others go on. We stood facing each other, only a few yards from the place where, little more than a week earlier, he had separated Henry and me. But things were very different.

I said, "How are you?"

It was not just a polite question. By now, if the Capping were going to fail, he would be feeling the pains and discomfort that would lead, in due course, to his becoming a Vagrant. He said, "I'm fine, Will."

I hesitated, and blurted out, "What was it like?"

He shook his head. "You know it's not permitted to talk about that. But I can promise you that you won't be hurt."

I said, "But why?"

"Why what?"

"Why should the Tripods take people away, and Cap them? What right have they?"

"They do it for our good."

"But I don't see why it has to happen. I'd sooner stay as I am."

He smiled. "You can't understand now, but you

will understand when it happens. It's . . ." He shook his head. "I can't describe it."

"Jack," I said, "I've been thinking." He waited, without much interest. "Of what you said—about the wonderful things that men made, before the Tripods."

"That was nonsense," he said, and turned and walked on to the village. I watched him for a time and then, feeling very much alone, made my way to the den.